the silver blade

Sally Gardner

SCHOLASTIC INC.

New York   Toronto   London   Auckland
Sydney   Mexico City   New Delhi   Hong Kong

First published in Great Britain in 2009 by Orion Children's Books

No part of this publication may be reproduced,
stored in a retrieval system, or transmitted in any form
or by any means, electronic, mechanical, photocopying, recording,
or otherwise, without written permission of the publisher. For information
regarding permission, write to Dial Books for Young Readers,
a division of Penguin Young Readers Group,
a member of Penguin Group (USA) Inc.,
345 Hudson Street, New York, NY 10014.

ISBN 978-0-545-29252-8

12 11 10 9 8 7 6 5 4 3 2 1   10 11 12 13 14 15/0

Printed in the U.S.A.   40

First Scholastic printing, September 2010

Designed by Nancy R. Leo-Kelly
Text set in Adobe Caslon Pro

For Judith,
I am the writer I am today because of you
and for that I am eternally grateful.
With your help and love I found my voice.

the silver blade

All that is necessary for the triumph of evil is that good men do nothing.

—*Bartlett's Familiar Quotations* (1968)

Prologue

There is no more terrifying a sight in all Paris than that of the guillotine. Never before has it been so easy to exterminate so many so quickly. Come rain or shine, come fog or snow, this indomitable killing machine is heedless of the weather or the passing seasons. It has no opinion of its victims or the number of times its blade is made to rise and fall in a single day.

It is as blind to the innocent as it is to the guilty; both receive the same dreadful, swift punishment. Never before has Death walked with such an assured step as it does in these dark days of the Reign of Terror.

The guillotine stands in the Place de la Révolution between the Garde-Meuble and the pedestal on which the Statue of Liberty has been erected. At night it is protected against the elements by a large canvas cloth tied fast with ropes. Even covered in its bloodstained winding sheet, it is a sight that inspires fear, and it is fear itself that like a contagious fever has taken hold of the city. It takes away all rational thought, bringing with it a delirium in which even your own shadow cannot be trusted. It spares neither the wise man nor the fool, the brave man nor the coward. Fear feeds on fear and, in March of 1794, it never goes hungry, for it is the devil's own supper.

Midnight in Paris and the bells ring out the hour, each peal skimming like a pebble over the surface of the city. Not a peaceful lullaby to end the day, but a troubled warning: "Lock your doors, close your shutters, and hide."

You can almost hear the universal prayer on every citizen's lips: that the morning light might find them still asleep in their bed; you can never tell which door the National Guard will come knock-knock-knocking on next, whose name will be written in that little black book.

"What's that noise?"

"There on the step."

"Who's coming in at the gate at such an hour?"

"Shh, listen. Isn't that the sound of boots upon the cobbles?"

"Did you hear that the seamstress was taken on the death cart only yesterday? Four children she leaves behind, orphaned."

"As long as it is not us."

"Quiet! What was that?"

"Pull your sheets about your ears, go to sleep, my dear."

Out there in this gated, barred, and locked city, a foggy mist rolls up the Seine from Rouen, clinging like a lady's veil just above the water line. It spreads into the narrow streets of the Place du Carrousel with its wretched hovels.

Here lives Remon Quint. Once key maker to the king, he sits in his tiny apartment regretting he hadn't left Paris when he had the chance. Now, blowing out the candle on his way to bed, to lie tossing and turning in a dreamless sleep, he wonders if it is all too late.

The mist rolls on to spy into cracks and crevices as it makes its way up the pickle of streets, by the ruins of a church, past the riding school, hanging like ghostly leaves on the rows of bare lime trees. In sight of the Tuileries Gardens, it lingers in the gutters, moving through the overcrowded slums where live the bird sellers, the brokers, jugglers and dentists, quacks and dog gelders. Gathering strength around Loup's butcher's shop, with its sign of a black iron pig that wheezes on rusty hinges, it sneaks up to look in through the chink in the shutters.

Madame Loup, the butcher's wife, is all alone tonight. The two people she dreads most in the world, her husband and her son, Anselm, are away from home. Where they are she doesn't know, she doesn't care. Lying in her wooden bed she dreams of her childhood, when she skipped barefoot through fields of sweet purple lavender, when the world was young and there still was hope.

In the Place de la Révolution, the moon has drawn back the heavy clouds shading its mournful gaze to see, emerging from the shadow of the guillotine, Count Kalliovski. He is tall, meticulously dressed, but his clothes offer little protection against such an inhospitable night as this. And though a wind is beginning to chase the mist away, making a threadbare thing of the vapors, it blows not one item of his clothing.

If you were a mouse, and a brave one at that, you might have the courage to creep closer, for those are expensive riding boots he wears, that have to them a red heel. Whoever this man is—whatever this man is—he is reckless indeed to wear so openly such decadent symbols of aristocracy as red heels, black silk breeches, and a silver-buttoned waistcoat embroidered with tiny silver skulls. He has red kid gloves, the color of poppies, his cravat is white as white can be, studded with a huge ruby pin like a single drop of blood. His coat collar rises to meet his hairline so that it looks as if his head is perched on, rather than connected to, his body. He appears to be a man of disjointed parts.

But it is his face beneath the hat that makes all the rest quite forgettable. Those black eyes do not look human, so dark and dead, eyes from which no light shines. His skin is like tallow wax, his hair, swept back, is black, his lips a red wound. This is a face of nightmares.

Kalliovski goes walking here every night, the smell of blood drawing him time and time again to the guillotine. It is like a fine wine to his nose, a perfume to savor. He takes a last deep breath, inhaling the scent of death before setting off toward the Pont Neuf. He walks without a shadow to mark his passing.

On the shoreline of the Seine, near the Louvre, he stops and whistles. He hears the wolfhound before he sees him. Balthazar is no longer the loyal dog he once was. He looks larger, his fangs longer and sharper, his claws have the sound of iron in them. His coat is mangy, grown odd in patches, he lacks the grace that once was so natural to him. He lacks the devotion to his master that once marked him out.

On the south side of the river they make their way up to the rue St. Jacques. Here in a passageway lives Maître Tardieu in his mole-like house. One miserable lantern lights his door. Kalliovski looks up at the shuttered window and wonders if the old lawyer knows where she is, and if he does, would he tell? It matters little. He will find Sido de Villeduval with the lawyer's help or without it. Nothing will stop him.

His motto is and always will be the same: Have no mercy, show no mercy.

Balthazar, restless to be gone, is at his master's side as they set off together down the deserted streets of the rue Jacob. They alone inhabit the night, specters of terror made visible, and Kalliovski revels in it. It has taken him time to accept that his power comes within the limitation of darkness. At the Place de Manon, Balthazar breaks away, howling, a sound that sends shivers down the spine of the living, a sound loud enough to wake the dead.

Kalliovski calls him back, but the dog has vanished. Turning on his heel, he curses as he walks up the rue des Couteaux until at last he reaches a shop with three dimly lit red lanterns glowing in the window.

Inside, the shelves are bare. But from behind the velvet curtain at the back a man appears, dressed from head to toe in black. Seeing his master he bows.

"Has it arrived, Serreto?" asks Kalliovski.

"Yes, master." He stands back to let Kalliovski pass, noticing that once again Balthazar is not with him.

At the back of the shop Kalliovski starts his descent, down the spiral stone stairs into the bowels of the earth where the air has a familiar smell of home, for seventy feet beneath the city is where the count now resides, in the catacombs. For years he planned his new abode, as if he had foreseen his own terrible destiny.

This is a palace as detached from reality as a ship from the shore. It is a world where Kalliovski makes the rules. He is its king. Now he sits in a wing-back chair studying the table before him.

In a frosted-glass dome, like a cake in a pastry shop, sits the waxwork head of the needy, greedy Marquis de Villeduval. It has been copied by Madame Tussaud from his death mask, for Kalliovski had only one request when he ordered the murder of the marquis on the eve of the September Massacre: that his face should remain unmarked.

"My mad marquis, what say you to your fate?" Kalliovski asks.

The wax head is silent, its watery blue eyes lost.

"Nothing to say, my dear foolish friend? Why, has the cat got your tongue?"

Kalliovski stretches his long legs, puts his poppy-red-gloved hands in front of him, dark threads spinning from his fingertips toward the wax head. His thoughts are a smoldering cauldron of revenge.

He will have Sido. This time there will be no escape. He will play his high card, and the game will be his.

The thin waxen lips of the late Marquis de Villeduval begin to move.

"The devil take you," he says.

Kalliovski throws back his head and laughs.

"He already has."

Chapter One

Yann Margoza was dressed as a vagabond in an old greatcoat that had seen better days, with a muffler wrapped around his neck, and a hat that had equally lived life to the full. Only if you saw his dark eyes with their unmistakable intensity would you ever have recognized him. His companion, Didier, was a huge bear-like figure of a man. The two had one thing in common: They possessed the ability to merge almost unseen with their surroundings.

They had been on the road now for three days and, although it was March, they could still feel winter's bitter breath in the wind. By late afternoon, an eerie yellow light flooded the woodland path. Soon pitch-blackness descended, as if the sun had been snuffed out. Thunder trumpeted in the approaching storm, a furious call to arms. Lightning tore at the sky. Finally the heavens opened.

Didier once more had the feeling that had troubled him ever since leaving Paris three days previously: They were being followed.

"Listen," he said.

"It's the wind," replied Yann.

"It sounded more like the howl of a wolf to me."

Yann kept walking, not listening, not looking, thinking only of Sido. The thought of her weighed so heavily. He barely noticed how cold, footsore, and hungry he was. Or that Didier was right.

Sido, Sido. In his mind's eye he could see her oval face, her blue eyes, her mass of wavy dark hair. He knew there was no other road his heart would travel but the road that led to her.

His thoughts had been thus engaged ever since leaving Paris; a tangled knot of desires. His mind drifted again to their first meeting all those years ago, at the Marquis de Villeduval's château. A fateful night that had changed the course of both their lives. His employer, Topolain the magician, had been shot dead by Count Kalliovski, and in the space of a few hours he had not only met his greatest adversary, but a young girl destined to be his greatest love, the keeper of his soul.

Now Kalliovski was long dead and Sido free, safe in England. No harm could come to her there. Why then did he have this feeling of foreboding?

Keeping his distance, Balthazar looked for telltale signs that he was on the right track. Mere mortals can't see in the dark without the light of a full moon or a lantern to guide them, especially not on such a stormy night as this, but the young man in the vagabond coat was different. Like his master, he walked with an almost supernatural confidence, as if it were broad daylight. Balthazar watched his every move, could smell his blood, hear his heart beat, almost taste his flesh.

He longed to find his old voice. He had been robbed of it; the only sounds left to him were those of a wild beast. He gave a mournful howl as hunger for the young man overwhelmed him.

"I'm right, aren't I?" said Didier, water dripping miserably off the brim of his hat. "There is something out there."

"Let's just keep walking," Yann shouted above the scream of the wind.

Didier reassured himself with the sound of his footsteps. One-two, one-two, the rhythm comforted him. He thought back to the time when Yann, spiriting a prisoner out of La Force, had left a silver blade from a street peddler's toy guillotine suspended over the sleeping head of a corrupt corporal. The weasel-faced man, instead of keeping his foul mouth shut, had boasted to one and all that the next time the Silver Blade, as he called him, came into his prison he would have his guts for garters, so he would. Didier, even in this bitter wind and with a stomach like an empty larder, felt comforted thinking of it. The corporal's boasting had backfired. He was sent to fight and was never heard of again, while the Silver Blade became a legend, a name whispered on the lips of despairing men, a name that brought hope to a city where hope had been banished.

No one who had been lucky enough to see Yann Margoza perform as the Harlequin in Paris at the Circus of Follies would ever in a thousand years of Sundays have suspected that he led a double life. But that is exactly what he did. The theater was a smokescreen for an altogether more subversive operation, that of helping citizens escape from the guillotine. Every member of Monsieur Aulard's theater company played his or her part in this dangerous venture, all knowing that their lives depended on Yann's talent.

Their backers were two English bankers: Charles Cordell, who lived in Paris, and Henry Laxton, with whom Yann had spent three years in London when younger. It was due to Laxton that he had received the education of an English gentleman. Both men had immediately seen the potential in Yann, demonstrated by the near-impossible feat of snatching Sido de Villeduval from the carriage of Count Kalliovski. Neither doubted that Yann could save many more lives, for he possessed courage and an ability to hold his nerve, no matter the situation in which he found himself.

That on its own would not have been enough, but Yann was of Gypsy blood, and had unusual skills. He was able to read people's thoughts, and had a gift for making clients forget quite how they had ever come to be rescued in the first place. In this way, his identity had remained something of a mystery. Without Yann's talents, the whole enterprise would have amounted to nothing more than a barrelful of good intentions. But with him, it had proved to be one of the most efficient operations in Paris.

Têtu, the dwarf, and Citizen Aulard, the theater

manager, worked together behind the scenes. It was their job these days to make sure that Yann and Didier had everything they needed to make each assignment a success. And recently, with the rumors of impending massacres once more circulating in Paris, their workload had doubled, if not tripled.

Yann and Didier's business, this time in Normandy, was to arrange the escape of the Duc de Bourcy and his family. It had been Têtu's decision that they should not travel from Paris by coach or on horseback, for such things would be remembered and could prove fatal. Instead he had insisted for their own safety that they take a boat up the Seine into the heartland of Normandy and go the rest of the way on foot.

What Têtu hadn't reckoned on was the weather. Originally they were only meant to be gone for five days, three of which had already passed, and they were yet to arrive. The delay put their whole operation at risk, leaving poor Monsieur Aulard and the rest of the company to cover for the Harlequin's absence.

"Did you hear it? Did you?" asked Didier, desperate not to be the only one to have heard the low, menacing growl. "Wasn't it you who told me that a wolf at the beginning of a journey is bad luck?"

"No," said Yann. "Russian Gypsies believe it is a good omen."

"I hope to God they're right," said Didier.

Lightning flashed, illuminating everything with looking-glass sharpness. They were in an abandoned graveyard, filled with silver birch trees standing guardian over the crumbling tombstones and broken, wingless angels. In the middle were the skeletal remains of a church, its roof long gone, only three walls preventing it from total collapse.

Yann moved toward it, quickly followed by Didier. Both were glad at last to have some protection, feeble as it was, from the spiteful wind, which hissed and wheezed around the masonry.

Looking into the bleakness of that devil-dark night, Yann heard no wolf howl. He heard nothing but his own gallow's-bird thoughts.

Why hasn't Sido replied to my letter? Three weeks and not a word. Perhaps I misunderstood her. What did she write?

Oh Yann, I long for thee, she had written.

Come back to me.

No, I didn't misunderstand her. We have hidden nothing from each other. Nothing. Except I have never told her I'm a Gypsy. I will when the time is right. Now I have told her what I should have told her ages ago, that I love her.

In the dark of the forest, in the light of his imagination, he pictured Sido as they had stood alone in the garden two years before, the smell of sea and autumn in the air, that moment when he had kissed her and held her. Why hadn't he had the courage to tell her then he loved her? Instead he had given her his precious talisman to wear, an amulet, the *baro seroeske sharkuni*, the shell of the shells. She had held it in her hands and brought it to her lips as he turned and walked away. She had whispered into it and he heard her words, soft as the waves kissing the seashore. Even then he could have changed everything. Why hadn't he? It was simple: He had wanted to earn her love, to prove, despite his Gypsy blood, that he was worthy of her.

It was after they had parted that he had started writing to her, frightened he might have lost her altogether. Soon their letters, dangerous as they were, became their lifeline, each more poignant, yet still skimming over what they longed to say. The last one he had received three weeks ago.

Why do I torment myself? I am a tightrope walker

over the Valley of Death. If I lose my balance I am lost. Sido's feet are on the ground. She owns all her tomorrows, has all her years to be arranged. A suitable husband, children. She lives in another country. Her time is measured by another clock. Her life has longitude and latitude. Mine has only now. If I live to see the end of the Terror, I will be a fortunate man.

He hit his hand hard against the side of the building. Didier looked at him.

"Are you all right?"

"Yes," mumbled Yann.

I love her. What is wrong with that? Everything, and I know it. It will take more than a revolution before society smiles on a Gypsy marrying a marquis's daughter.

"Can you hear it now?" said Didier.

Hell, why haven't I been paying better attention? Didier is right. And a wolf at the beginning of a journey is not a good omen to French Gypsies.

"Yes," said Yann.

Didier had started shivering. "I don't like this place. It may sound daft, but my feet don't feel as though they're standing on solid ground."

Yann had the same feeling.

"Is it man or beast?" asked Didier, blowing into his mittened hands.

"I'm not sure."

Didier looked about nervously. "That's not like you," he whispered. "Can't you see none of those threads of light thingumajigs you always see?"

The threads of light, thought Yann. Of course. Why are there no threads of light? Even tables, chairs, have straight ones. Everything has threads of light . . . except the dead.

"Shh!" said Yann.

A twig snapped.

Didier stood stock-still, feeling the hairs prickle on the back of his neck. All around him was an endless, smothering, velvety blackness.

"It's something evil. I feel it," he whispered to Yann.

"It belongs to the darkness, not the light, that's all I know."

They walked through the graveyard, Didier clinging to Yann's coat, fearful of losing him. They passed the broken remains of a large dovecote and emerged in the formal gardens of a château. The rain turned to icy sleet as they made their way up the stone steps. On either side of the front door stood statues of roaring lions, their mouths open, water dripping off their chiseled teeth.

Yann looked back the way they'd come. It was then he heard her voice, caught on the wind's breath.

Run. The devil's own is on your trail.

He knew that voice, a ghost calling to him on a soulless night.

At that moment he saw it on the gravel drive—the liquid black shape of a great dog or wolf. It stayed watching him before finally moving into the shadow of the gardens. Balthazar, thought Yann. Kalliovski's dog. But that was impossible—for he, like his master, was dead, killed by the mob on the Pont Neuf.

He shuddered, remembering what Têtu had told him: That was the day the devil had gone walking, searching for one irredeemable soul to blow his fiery life into. There could be no man more deserving of the devil's attention than Count Kalliovski. If he was alive, then no one was safe.

Sido was not safe.

Chapter Two

The Duc de Bourcy was a tall, thin man whose face had been etched gray by worry and fever. He was standing in a chamber of elegant proportions that was awash with furniture, as if a great tide had rushed through, gathering all in its wake. Sofas, chairs, tables, cabinets, screens, and writing desks stood forlornly. Scattered in between them was a collection of clocks, ticking loudly, hoping to keep time from running out, for the hour was fast approaching when all this would be swept away.

The duke hoped—no, his fervent prayer was—that he and his family would be saved before the National Guard arrived to arrest him. He'd been waiting over a week for Cordell's man to turn up, but no one had come. And every day the situation seemed more hopeless. Like a drowning man, he held fast to the belief that Charles Cordell would not abandon him, that he would, as promised, send his very best man.

His beloved château, unlike those of many of his acquaintance, had so far been spared the ravages of the Revolution. Not that attempts hadn't been made. The worst had happened shortly after the storming of the Bastille.

On a summer's day the villagers, fired with revolutionary zeal, and armed with pitchforks, swords, old kitchen knives, and axes, had marched up the long, slow, steep hill ready to storm the château. The duke, on being told they were coming to destroy his property, had instructed that his cellars be emptied and wine, cheese, and bread left in baskets outside the gates.

When the villagers arrived hot and thirsty after their long, slow, steep march, they were delighted to see that their needs had been so well catered for. Having eaten and drunk their fill, they began to forget why they had come in the first place. One of the tenant farmers even praised the duke. As the sun went down, they drank the last of the wine and rolled back to the village, singing songs as if they had spent the day at a country fete.

After that the duke had believed himself safe. So it seemed a cruel twist of fate to find that a letter he had written to a friend abroad had been intercepted and found its way into Robespierre's hands. A warrant for his arrest was issued, and he'd wasted no time in asking for urgent help from his banker and good friend, Charles Cordell.

Now, pacing back and forth, his movements were constricted by the clutter of furniture. He looked up relieved when Didier and Yann entered the room, and went to greet Didier.

"Monsieur, I cannot tell you how pleased I am to see you. There is no time to be lost."

Didier indicated Yann and said politely but firmly, "This is the gentleman you are after."

The duke turned to look at Yann. An expression of incredulity spread over his face.

"You?" he said, making it sound like an accusation. "You! *Mon dieu*, Lord above preserve us! Has Cordell lost his mind, sending me a young lad?"

"My age shouldn't concern—"

"This is ridiculous," interrupted the duke. "I have wasted precious time waiting for—what? For you two?"

His hands shook. He stopped in mid-stride and by the light of the fire, they could see that he was not a well man.

"Have you brought the papers?"

"Yes."

"Then we must leave without delay." The duke moved to ring a bell.

Yann reached it before him.

"No."

"What the—?" The duke turned on him. "I have given an order!"

"No," repeated Yann calmly. "You are not in a position to give me orders. You will do what you are told; otherwise I won't be taking any of you. Do you understand me?"

"I don't want your help then! I didn't pay Cordell a small fortune to be insulted. Oh, *mon dieu, mon dieu!*" He stopped, throwing his hands up in despair. "Time is of the essence. Give me the papers, sir."

Yann stayed where he was.

"You are dismissed. I shall not require your assistance."

"It's tempting," said Didier, "very tempting indeed."

"I will not be spoken to like this," said the duke,

sweat glimmering on his forehead. "You will respect what I say, do you hear me?"

Yann laughed. "Do you think the Bluecoats will respect you when they come to arrest you? That they will bow three times and call you by your full title? No, you'll be treated worse than a farm animal. Without our help, I can promise you, you will not make it to England."

"Are you threatening me?"

"No," said Yann.

"Cordell gave me his word that he would send only his best man to help us, a gentleman. You, sir, are no gentleman." The duke stopped, overcome by a fit of coughing.

The door of the antechamber opened and the duchess came in with her two children. She was still a young woman, elegant in bearing and solemn in appearance. Once, no doubt, she had possessed beauty; the remnants of it remained in her steady gray eyes. Cool in her troubled face, they shone with an iron will.

Both children had the same solemn expression. The younger, Louis, seemed about five. He had a mop of blond curls and large brown eyes, while his brother, Hugo, looked like a miniature version of the duke.

"I beg you, Raoul, calm yourself. This is going to

make you ill again," said the duchess, leading her husband to a sofa. Defeated, he sat next to his wife. She took his hand gently in hers. Hugo sat beside his mother while Louis leaned back on his papa's legs, sucking his thumb.

To break the awkward silence, Didier said, "If you don't mind me saying, there's a lot of furniture in this room."

"There are looters who steal treasures and have them smuggled to England," replied the duchess, "so we have taken the precaution of keeping our valuables up here with us."

"We've been informed that the Bluecoats are in on it. There's a certain Sergeant Berigot who runs the operation with the help of an Englishman. Anyway," said the duke miserably, "what does any of it matter? It's too late. We'll never escape, not now."

"Please, young man," said the duchess, turning toward Yann, "don't be offended or think us ungracious. My husband has been very ill. So many terrible things have happened. Friends of ours have been arrested, their homes destroyed. Some have been executed."

"I can assure you that Monsieur Cordell knew what he was doing when he sent us. We will leave in the morning once the storm has subsided. I advise you, sir, get some rest. You are all going to need it."

"I think I should inform you that I shall not be traveling with you," said the duchess.

"That's madness!" said Didier. "Monsieur Cordell told us the whole family would be leaving."

"I know that's what we said," replied the duke. "But after a great deal of anguish we have made a decision. My wife is going to stay here and divorce me. It's the only way we have of saving the estate."

Yann stood dumbfounded. Didier was right to call this madness.

"There's a loophole in the law," the duke went on. "If she divorces me on the grounds of my being an émigré, all my property goes to her and we hope, when this is over, we can be reunited."

"*Maman*, please come," cried Louis, throwing his arms around his mother's neck. "I don't want to leave you alone."

"My darling," said his mother, "we are doing this so that one day we can all be together again."

The duke interrupted. "I'm damned if I'll let this land be given to the Convention to be wasted and squandered. It has been in our family for generations."

"Still, it's lunatic—"

"Quiet, Didier," said Yann, seeing tears roll down the faces of the little boys. "Perhaps the children should go to bed."

The duchess rang a bell. It was answered by a maid whose wooden clogs sounded loudly on the parquet floor.

Louis and Hugo clung to their mother. Yann knelt beside them and from behind Louis's ear he conjured a spinning top.

Louis's eyes lit up. "Do it again!"

"Now, watch carefully and you might learn something," said Yann. And from behind Hugo's ear he brought out a wooden soldier.

"More, more!" shouted Louis and Hugo, clapping their hands.

"In the morning," said Yann softly.

The duchess kissed the two boys. "Be good and go to bed."

After they had gone, the duke stood up unsteadily. He looked like a bowed willow, bent by the strong winds of troubled times.

"My wife," he said, taking the duchess's hand and kissing it, "is determined to stay here, and all I will add to that is God bless her. We will leave in the morning with you, sir. I see that we have no choice but to put our trust in you. Until then, *adieu*."

He left the room, leaning on his wife's arm.

Didier stood, bewildered, while the clocks began to strike the half hour.

"She can't possibly mean it," he said, finally, as the last chime died. "Lord knows why I should care one way or the other. What angers me is that we risked everything to get here, to be insulted, and now we'll be late getting back, leaving Têtu and Citizen Aulard in a predicament, for the sake of a couple of numskulls with whom I have no sympathy. For that matter, I've no sympathy with any aristocrat foolish enough to put more store in property than people."

"Be careful, Didier. It's not that simple," Yann said. "The word *aristocrat* has been redefined; it includes merchants, bankers, tradesmen, clerks, lawyers. I tell you this much: Soon the sans-culottes will have you arrested for addressing someone as *monsieur*."

"For a slip of the tongue?" said Didier.

"You think not? Use the word *monsieur* in public and I assure you that you'll be arrested for hankering after the old regime. *Citizen* is, after all, the most honorable of titles; the definition of a virtuous man."

Didier regarded him for a moment, then, "Look," he said, "it's simple. This is a battle between the haves and the have-nots."

Yann laughed. "I think it's much more complicated than that, and the green-eyed monster plays a larger part in this drama than you give him credit for."

"What green-eyed monster?" asked Didier.

"Mr. Trippen, an actor and my tutor in London, loved quoting Shakespeare. One of his favorites was *Othello*: 'Beware, my lord, of jealousy; it is the green-eyed monster which doth mock the meat it feeds on.' Most men, if they're honest, would like to live in this house, to have servants, to own land."

"Not you, not me."

"We, my friend, might well be the exceptions," said Yann, going over to the window and opening one of the shutters.

Outside, the storm raged and the rain slashed at the windowpane, making it impossible for Yann to see anything but his own reflection.

Didier shrugged. "I would choose life over property any time," he said, unbuttoning his coat and hanging it over one of the many chairs in front of

33

the fire. He took off his boots and rested them on the grate to dry.

"You should do the same," he said, looking at Yann still wrapped in his sodden greatcoat. "I'll go and find something to eat."

Yann stood by the fire. Steam rose from his soaking clothes.

How many times have I arrived at a château just like this one, he thought to himself, to be greeted in the same dismissive manner? I suppose everyone's idea of a savior is different. I am never what anyone expects. The duke spoke the truth.

My mother was a Gypsy, she told fortunes, had the gift of working the threads of light. She danced for fine gentlemen. What was the rhyme Têtu used to tell me?

O, I am not of the gentle clan,
I'm sprung from the Gypsy tree,
And I will be no gentleman,
But a Romany free.

It matters not. No, it matters. It always has mattered.

Yann leaned forward, his forehead cooled by the marble mantelpiece. Looking down into the burning city of coals, he knew his airs and graces had been hard won.

"He is a good man," came the soft voice of the duchess. She was standing behind him. "It's just that we had been expecting the Silver Blade. Foolish, I know. It's only a name, but his reputation had led us to believe that once he arrived we would be safe."

Yann didn't move. He kept his eyes fixed on the burning coals.

"The Silver Blade is just a name on the street. He doesn't exist."

"I believe he does. For all our sakes, I pray he does," replied the duchess. "I am told that when someone escapes or disappears from under the eyes of the police, they look frantically for the small silver blade, suspended as if by a spider's thread."

"A fairy tale, nothing more," said Yann.

"We need fairy tales, or some belief in magic. Without that, aren't we all lost?"

"Perhaps," replied Yann.

"Monsieur Cordell told us you helped Sidonie de Villeduval escape."

At the sound of her name, Yann turned to the duchess. His dark eyes studied her face intently before he asked, "You know the marquis's daughter?"

"No, we knew her uncle, Armand. He was one of my husband's best friends and instrumental in forming his philosophy toward his tenants. A kinder and more considerate man would be hard to imagine. His was a terrible loss. Tell me, was it truly you who rescued Sidonie?"

Yann nodded.

She went up to him and kissed his hand. "God bless you," she said. "I, unlike you, monsieur, believe in fairy stories." She turned to leave. Pausing at the door she asked, "Have you seen the guillotine?"

"Yes."

"I am told that the blade falls so fast the mob feels cheated of the spectacle. Is that so?"

"It is indeed very swift."

"How absurd is life when it is valued so cheaply," she said, closing the door behind her.

Didier returned with a plate piled high with bread and meat, and carrying a jug of wine and two glasses.

"A feast, and the good thing is there's more where that comes from," he said. Pulling a chair up near the fire, he started to eat. "What are you waiting for, Yann? You must be famished. Come on."

From outside, a howl like a wolf's penetrated the room. Didier stopped eating.

"Did you hear that?"

Yann nodded.

"It gives me the shudders. Sounds like it comes from the graveyard."

Just then all the clocks in the room began to chime. Father Time, who knows the hour of each man's death, was beating out the last minutes of the day and still above the cacophony of noise that dreadful howl could be heard.

Whatever it was that lurked out there in the dead of midnight, Yann felt certain of one thing. It was waiting for him.

Tick-tock, tick-tock.

Chapter Three

Mr. Tull sat in the corner of L'Auberge des Pêcheurs, not far from the village of Greville. Outside, the sign creaked in the wind and the round bottle-glass windows rattled. Such was the battering the storm was giving this humble dwelling that, had it not been for the solidity of the floor, he might have believed himself to be at sea and likely to hit the rocks at any moment.

Mr. Tull, who was slumped at a table beside the fire, was much changed of late. Gone was the stocky figure with the bulldog manner. In its place sat a haunted-looking man whose bulbous eyes darted constantly to the door, as if whoever he was expecting might have already slipped past him unseen.

"Another cognac," he shouted. The spiteful wind hissed its way in through the many cracks. The tallow candles flickered and faltered. The innkeeper, placing a bucket on the floor to catch the raindrops from the leaking ceiling, glanced at his one and only customer.

"Be with you in a moment, citizen," he said, nodding toward his daughter to go and serve their customer.

Mr. Tull, half watching from the corner of his eye, could tell she had refused. He shifted uneasily into the shadows, realizing that she was frightened of him.

Maybe I have the mark of the devil on me, and she can see its stain, he thought wretchedly. My life would be good—I would be good—if only I could rid myself of my master.

He shuddered and set his mind on more cheerful subjects, such as the cottage he had just purchased by the sea in Kent, where he planned to retire and grow cabbages, a morsel of consolation for all his hard work.

The innkeeper, apologizing for the delay, came over with the cognac. Mr. Tull snatched the bottle. "Are you expecting anyone else, citizen?"

"Two more, and we shall want dinner."

The innkeeper was without doubt wondering what in God's name had brought this man out on such a night. What had brought him was furniture, the stealing and shipping of stolen goods—and a very profitable business it had turned out to be. Furniture, unlike would-be émigrés, didn't fuss or suffer from seasickness. Furniture wasn't prone to weeping and wailing. Furniture always kept its price and could be satisfactorily explained away.

He had had a tip-off from Sergeant Berigot that the Duc de Bourcy was going to be arrested tomorrow. If he wanted to break into the château, he had been told, best to do it before the Bluecoats decided to make kindling out of the duke's possessions.

His partners in crime these days were the butcher, Citizen Loup, and his unexpectedly beautiful seventeen-year-old son, Anselm. They had first met by chance at a café in the Palais Royal. Citizen Loup was at the time feeling much aggrieved, for he had been reprimanded for taking a chair from a château that was to be burned to the ground.

"Surely there must be some perks for tearing down the symbols of oppression? I only took what rightfully belonged to me."

Mr. Tull had bought him a drink, and by the end of the evening the three had agreed to go into partnership.

Tomorrow, thought Mr. Tull, stretching his legs toward the fire, he would be on his way to England, accompanying the duke's possessions to an auction house. He wouldn't be returning, not for a while. His master had business for him in London. He wanted him to locate a certain young lady, one with whom Mr. Tull had had dealings before—Sido de Villeduval. And locating people was what Mr. Tull was good at.

He sat there, waiting, watching, drinking as another leak in the ceiling appeared. Drip-drop, drip-drop, water inside, water outside, everywhere water.

At that moment, the wind took hold of the door and threw it wide open, blowing the sawdust off the floor.

The innkeeper rushed forward, cursing; then, seeing the imposing figure of Citizen Loup and his son in the doorway, he backed away.

"What kept you so long?" said Mr. Tull, rising to greet them. The butcher, a beast of a man with pig eyes in a ruddy face, entered, followed by Anselm. The boy's beauty shone like a beacon in this dimly lit inn, making him appear as if he had come from another world entirely.

"*Merde alors*, have you noticed the weather, *rosbif*? We've had the devil of a job getting here," said the butcher, shaking the water from his coat like a dog. "I hope it's going to be worth it."

He sat down and ordered a bottle of wine, while Anselm went over to the innkeeper's flustered daughter, who couldn't believe her good fortune that the wind should have blown in one so handsome.

Mr. Tull watched the lad walk away. There was something about that young man that made his flesh creep. On the whole, he thought to himself, he liked his fellow thieves and villains to look as devious as the trade they performed. Like Citizen Loup: What you saw was what you got. Angels made him uneasy.

Anselm had grown up looking more beautiful than many a young girl. His skin had not one blemish to spoil its perfection; his cheeks possessed the blush of a fine autumn apple.

He had learned at an early age the power his beauty had over people. Even when he was naughty he was rarely scolded. No one could quite bring themselves to believe a child with such angelic looks could do anything wrong. The only person he had failed to impress had been the downtrodden Madame Loup.

She knew the truth of his birth. He was not of her flesh and blood. He had been abandoned in a basket of putrid animal entrails at the back of the shop. The butcher had wanted to slaughter the infant, but she had pleaded to be allowed to take it to the nuns.

Then something odd had happened. The butcher had seen in the baby's yellow eyes another wolf. And wolves don't kill their own kind. The butcher had threatened to slit Madame Loup's throat if she ever told the boy the truth. He soon forgot he was not his son; she never could. All her babies had been stillborn, their eyes never opened, their hunger for life a whisper in a candle flame, snuffed out. This baby had been ravenous for life and clung to it with a tyrannical grip that repulsed her.

As a child, Anselm had become fascinated by his father's trade, saw him as a giant, an ogre who possessed an almost mythical power over life and death. The butcher saw in Anselm a kindred spirit, someone worthy of inheriting the business.

Few people can claim they are born into the right period of history. Most of us have to make do with the times we find ourselves in. This could not be said of Anselm, nor for that matter his father, for never had a revolution come at a better time. It liberated them completely from any morals they might have had. In any other age, both would have been called murderers. Instead, the September Massacre had raised father and son, the beast and the beauty, to the status of heroes. They had been called the Spirit of the Revolution.

"How long have we got before the château's raided?" asked the butcher.

"My sources tell me tomorrow, about nine o'clock in the morning," said Mr. Tull, relighting his clay pipe.

Anselm returned and sat down, while the inn-keeper's daughter, having lost her fear of Mr. Tull and blushing bright red, served them their supper.

The rain battered at the windows, and the wind listened through the cracks to what the three crooks had to say. They agreed there would be no point leaving the warmth of the inn until the worst of the storm had abated.

The plates were finally cleared and another bottle of cognac placed on the table. Anselm stoked the fire so it roared and hissed, while his father settled back in his chair, tired after their journey, annoyed that the pain in his chest had come back. He closed his eyes and fell fast asleep, snoring loudly.

Mr. Tull on the other hand was wide-awake. He

poured himself another glass. With no one to steady his hand he'd drunk more than enough.

"Pa tells me that you also work for a very mysterious gentleman indeed. Is that true?"

Mr. Tull couldn't remember ever having had a conversation with Anselm before. Usually the boy looked bored rigid by everything he had to say.

"I do indeed have another job," he said, taking from his pocket a rather fine watch.

Anselm still had his bewitching eyes fixed on Mr. Tull, who felt somewhat uneasy at the intense look of innocence that this young lad's face possessed. He snapped the watch shut. Even though he had never learned how to tell the time, he hoped it gave him a look of authority.

"Come on, have a drink with me. Or can't you take your liquor?"

"It's not that, Mr. Tull," said Anselm, smiling. "I don't want any more." Instead, he lifted the bottle and filled Mr. Tull's glass to the brim.

Mr. Tull raised his glass and started to sing,

"Old Nick is ailing
He's complaining tonight."

"So tell me about your master, then," said Anselm.

"Old Nick is ailing," sniggered Mr. Tull. "I wish he was. Many men would pay high to know about my master."

He leaned toward Anselm. "It's as dark as Hades down there. Hell don't burn bright with flames, no, it damn well don't. It's dark. It smells of dead men's bones. I should know. I work for a man who lives under the city of Paris, in the catacombs."

Anselm knew of the catacombs all right, a grim network of tunnels where thousands of bodies from the September Massacre had been dumped, seventy feet below the city. He couldn't imagine who would choose to live down there.

"He sounds like a strange one, he does."

"I suppose that if you can't stand the light," said Mr. Tull, letting out a laugh, "it's the best place for you."

"What? He *lives* in one of them dark tunnels like a rat?"

"I'll tell you something that will shock you," said Mr. Tull. "There is nothing dark about the apartment my master lives in."

"What do you mean, apartment? There are only tunnels and dripping water down there. It's where the dead go to rot."

"That's what you think. My master is one of the richest men in Paris—" He stopped for a moment. His words were beginning to slur. "He's had the most stupendous set of chambers built for himself. Lined, they are, all in human bones covered in gold leaf. The chambers are lit by thousands of candles. He has a lake and a ballroom down there! What do you say to that?"

Anselm wasn't sure whether to believe Mr. Tull, but he didn't think the old rogue had the imagination to make up such a thing.

"Why does he live down there then, if he's so rich?"

"I told you, didn't I, he doesn't like the light." Mr. Tull finished his glass. "What—you still not drinking?"

"Want to keep a clear head for the work, don't I, Mr. Tull," Anselm said, smiling. "You, on the other hand, don't have to worry."

"You're right, lad. Now, what was I saying?"

"You were telling me the reason for your master living down in the catacombs, remember?" Anselm again lifted the bottle of cognac, and drained it into Mr. Tull's glass.

"Yes, that's right, he got hurt, didn't he. Him and that dog of his got taken down there. Has to stay out of the light . . . Shall I tell you a secret, boy?"

Anselm nodded.

Mr. Tull's vision had lost focus now. Anselm appeared more angelic than ever, a halo of light shining around his head. Yes, he was an angel come to save him.

"Will you forgive me my trespasses?" said Mr. Tull, his frog-like eyes beginning to close.

"I will if you tell me your secret," said Anselm, leaning forward.

Mr. Tull shook himself awake. Secret? What secret?

What had he let slip to the boy? Sitting bolt upright, he said, "You forget about the Seven Sisters Macabre, you just forget about them, all right? I never said a word!"

He had a feeling he was saying things that in the sober light of day he would come to regret.

Anselm, fearing that Mr. Tull might fall asleep at any moment, asked, "What sisters?"

"They're half-alive and always dead," Mr. Tull mumbled, his eyes slipping closed again.

Anselm was beginning to feel like throttling the old drunk. He must have made up the sisters, he thought, to stop me asking about his master.

"Is he a young man?"

"Who?" said Mr. Tull.

"Your master."

"No, he claims to be as old as Charlemagne."

"Is he the Silver Blade?"

Mr. Tull was beginning to feel too tired to be bothered with any more questions. He yawned and said, "Let's talk about something different. Have you a sweetheart?"

"Lots," said Anselm quickly. "No, really, Mr. Tull, I am interested in what you have to say, honest I am."

"Sure you are. I'm just going to close my eyes. You should do the same," Mr. Tull muttered. His French was never good even at the best of times.

"Who is your master? What's his name?" asked Anselm.

Mr. Tull's lids closed over his eyes. His head lolled forward as a drunken sleep began to overtake him.

Anselm, desperate now to know, asked again. "Your master, what name did you say?"

Gently Mr. Tull began to snore.

Anselm shook him and asked the question again.

More asleep than awake, Mr. Tull sighed. "My master is the devil."

Chapter Four

If you were an owl that evening, swooping over the wind-tossed trees, you would see with your round wise eyes the château of the Duc de Bourcy and the surrounding woods spread out beneath you. And there, where the trees are thickest, you might catch the glimmer of a light bouncing from one bare branch to another. And if, from curiosity, you were to fly closer still, you would not be surprised to see Mr. Tull driving his hired cart and horse, with the butcher sitting hunched beside him while Anselm, feet dangling, sat at the back. They were making their way unobserved, or so they hoped, toward the château.

The success of these robberies lay in Mr. Tull's ability to plan for all emergencies. In this alone he was neat and methodical. The cart carried blankets, a saddle, some rope, pistols, an axe, and his house-breaking tools wrapped in a leather pouch. Never did he undertake a job without an accurate layout of the château he was going to raid. This one had proven easy. A servant who had once been in the duke's employment had furnished him with detailed plans.

Mr. Tull and his two accomplices saw the work they did as a necessity: not so much breaking the law, more supporting the Revolution. After all, Citizen Loup and his son were thought of as heroes in their community. If tonight they were to stumble upon anyone who was pig-headed enough to stand in their way, they would kill him without a moment's regret.

The three were soaked through and none of them was in a particularly good humor, each for very different reasons. Mr. Tull had drunk more than he should have and his head was throbbing badly. Anselm was fed up at having to leave the innkeeper's daughter, who had so willingly given of her kisses. As for the butcher, the pain in his chest was even worse.

"You got everything you need?" asked Mr. Tull as the cart came to a halt. "The clocks—remember the clocks. Tall ones, small ones, as long as they're ornate. And don't forget the paintings, of course."

"Shut up, you fat gutted dog," said the butcher. "We've been over this more times than I care to say. What, you don't trust me? Think yourself better than me, do you? Think I wouldn't recognize the hen painter?"

"No, no. And the painter's *name* is Poussin," said Mr. Tull.

"I don't care what the scum was called. Be careful how you talk to me, citizen. Remember, *rosbif*, we're all equal."

"And I'm an Englishman."

"You'll be a dead one if you don't shut that potato trap of yours."

Mr. Tull felt rattled. Never had the butcher been quite as touchy as he was tonight. The horse snorted and stamped its hooves.

"Keep that animal quiet, *rosbif*, if that's not too taxing a job for you."

The butcher pulled up the collar of his coat and stuck his favorite pig-killing knife into his belt, muttering to himself as he walked toward the château.

"All this wealth in the hands of the stinking rich, who've done nothing for it but feed off the carcasses of the poor."

Anselm laughed.

"What's so funny?" said the butcher, turning on him.

"Nothing, nothing, Pa. I just agree with you, that's all."

The butcher's rage was more with himself than anyone else. The pain in his chest was worse than ever. He waited outside by the window, keeping a lookout, while Anselm went around to the main door.

Locks had never been a problem. Anselm enjoyed breaking them and had found ways to make even the strongest yield. With the use of a few good tools he managed to open the ornate carved door. Once inside, he stood in the hall, listening to see if anyone was awake.

Calmly he lit his lantern, then studied the plans. The large double doors at the end of the hall creaked loudly as he slipped through them. For a moment he wasn't sure he was in the right room. Lifting up his lantern he could see quite clearly that it was empty. There was not a clock, not a painting, not a stick of furniture to be seen.

Outside, the butcher was impatient to get started. Seeing a light through a crack in the shutters, he tapped on them.

"Hurry up, what are you waiting for? I'm half frozen out here."

Anselm forced the window open. The butcher, unlike his son, was not light on his feet. The din he made heaving his ample frame over the windowsill was the noise that gave them away.

Yann had been standing by an upstairs window. He saw a light flicker in the trees, then disappear.

"Come here, Didier," Yann said. "What do you see?"

Didier stared into the darkness. "Nothing. But I don't have a good feeling about this business. Never have had, not since I first heard that creature howl."

"Shh!" said Yann. "Did you hear that?"

"What?" said Didier. "This place makes more noises than a creaking galleon. Which one of the many in particular caught your attention?"

They both stood stock-still, listening.

Now Didier heard it as well. "Maybe it's a servant who couldn't sleep, just—"

He stopped. This time the sound was unmistakable.

A window had been forced open. The noise was coming from downstairs. Yann moved quickly toward the door.

Didier went over to his knapsack and brought out his pistol. "I tell you this much: I'll be mighty pleased to see dawn."

"So will I," replied Yann, opening the door. "You stay here. I'll go and see what's going on."

The butcher took the lantern and looked around the room.

"Where're the clocks, then?"

"That's what I wondered," said Anselm. "Do you think the Bluecoats have been already?"

"No," said the butcher. "Mark my words, the tyrant of oppression has taken his furniture upstairs. I'll go investigate, and you go back and get that thick-skulled rascal Tull here now. We're going to need all hands on deck."

Anselm climbed out of the window. He had started to make his way toward the cart when he heard a muffled shout. Turning, he saw the room ablaze with light—more light than one lantern could make. Silently he moved closer, pistol in hand, the trigger pulled back. Peering around the side of the window, he saw a young man standing by the door. Anselm quickly pressed himself against the cold brick wall. Slowly he dared to take another look. He had a strange feeling that he had seen this person before. Whoever he was, he didn't stand a chance against his pa.

The young man was unarmed. The butcher charged toward him, wielding his pig-killing knife, ready to split his head open like a watermelon. Anselm felt a thrill of delight at his father's power, at the inevitability of it all.

Then something happened. Something that Anselm couldn't fathom. Something that went against all logic. For a start, the young man didn't move. He didn't duck or dive as the butcher came for him. Far from it. He had a smile on his face and his hands raised before him like a conjuror. In that instant the butcher's knife was snatched from his grasp—but instead of landing with an enormous clang on the floor, it hung suspended in midair.

Anselm felt the stir of something he had rarely experienced. Fear. It crippled him and fascinated him. He watched in awe as his father's feet left the ground, lifted up as if by some invisible threads.

And then the memory, diamond bright, came to him: On the parapet of the Pont Neuf on the first day of the September Massacre, he had seen this very same young man in a sky-blue coat. Like an avenging angel, he had unleashed an invisible force causing knives and axes to fly from their owners' hands. A man had been lifted high in the air and thrown into the mob. In the mayhem of that moment he had childishly believed in the impossible, before the grimness of the bloody day crushed all such infantile thoughts.

Now, witnessing this magic close up, he knew he would give his soul to possess such power.

Never had Anselm been so aware of his own mortality as he was in those few seconds before his father's diseased and swollen heart burst. The butcher's lifeless body was left hanging, a worthless lump of meat.

Didier, pistol drawn, rushed down the stairs the minute he heard the commotion, followed by the duke. They entered the chamber ready to do battle, but they froze when they saw the butcher, his head lolling and his eyes glassy with fright. Blood trickled down his chin and dripped onto the polished parquet floor.

"He's dead," said Didier, looking up at him.

"All I did was suspend him," said Yann.

"He must have had a heart attack," said Didier, closing the window and pulling together the shutters.

The duke stared at Yann as if seeing him for the first time. He bowed deeply. "I hope you will accept my sincere apologies for my rudeness to you earlier. I would never have imagined that one so young could wield such power. I see now that Cordell did indeed send me his best man."

Anselm, wet and trembling, crept away until he reached the nearest copse.

The wind blew and the rain fell. Shadows loomed. Anselm's heart was in his mouth. Too terrified to move, he pushed his nails deep into the bark of a tree trunk.

A howl pierced the night as a crack of light broke through and the hope of a new day could be seen. Anselm stood rigid with terror. He saw on the ground the shadow of a mighty hound, black as coal, liquid as molten iron. Then it vanished among the trees, chasing the tail of darkness. In a blind funk of panic, with rain and sweat rolling down his face, Anselm finally saw the light on the cart.

Mr. Tull was feeling very uneasy. He took a swig from his flask to steady his nerves. What the hell was keeping them?

"My pa's dead," said Anselm.

Mr. Tull nearly jumped out of his skin. "I didn't see you coming. What did you say?"

"My pa's dead."

"Think you can make a fool of me, you double-crossing rogues?" He jumped down, grabbed Anselm by his muffler, and pushed him against the cart. "You think I buy your meddlesome mischief?"

Anselm gasped for air. Mr. Tull had a strong grip.

"No, no, honest, I tell you he . . . Pa was . . . It was like he was hanging on an invisible rope! I ain't making it up, honest I ain't, and I tried to get here sooner, but I think there's a wolf out there."

At the word *wolf,* Mr. Tull let go. Anselm pulled the muffler from around his neck so that he might breathe better, and seeing Mr. Tull untying the horse from the cart cried, "Wait! Don't leave me here, please!"

Mr. Tull, suddenly stone-cold sober, put the saddle on the horse, grateful that he had had the foresight to bring it with him.

"What're you doing?" said Anselm. "We can't leave my pa like that."

Mr. Tull, ghost white, said, "You sure it was a wolf?"

"Yes . . . No . . . I don't know. It was a shadow . . . but my pa is inside there, dead."

"A shadow," Mr. Tull repeated to himself as he mounted.

"Please, Mr. Tull, what are you doing?"

"What does it look like? Getting out of here while I still can. If you value your life I advise you to do the same."

"But what about—"

Mr. Tull wasn't listening. He had already started off at a gallop.

The storm was dying, the sky striped ruby red. Anselm, his nerves torn to shreds, walked, baffled, toward the breaking day.

Chapter Five

From the color of dawn next morning, one might have suspected the gods of fighting a gargantuan battle, wounding the sun itself, for the sky ran bloodred, saturating the earth in scarlet. In this raw new day, Didier carried the body of the butcher like a slab of meat on his massive shoulders.

They buried the butcher under the rotten floorboards in the derelict dovecote, among white discarded feathers and dried-up bird droppings. Only the wind heard them, only the crows saw the butcher's final resting place.

"May the Lord have mercy on him," said the duke.

"And may the worms be spared the blackguard's foul flesh," added Didier, brushing the mud from his coat.

Yann said nothing. He knew there were no words

to save the butcher, for he could see, standing among the pink of the beech trees, the ghosts of his many victims.

Like the dawn itself, each was stained bloodred. They stood watching, waiting, ready to greet their murderer.

Yann doubted the butcher would find peace eternal beyond the grave.

The household was already awake by the time they got back, muddy and wet. The fires had been lit, and hot chocolate, bread, and butter waited for them on the table.

Yann took no notice of these niceties. He didn't even take off his coat. Instead, he asked for three of the duke's fastest horses to be made ready. They must leave without delay.

"Surely you will eat something?" asked the duchess.

"There is no time," said Yann. "We should have left over an hour ago. If we fail to make the tide, the boatman won't wait for us and all hope of escape will be lost."

The duchess understood the need for urgency. She embraced her husband, both gathering courage, as their sons were brought down the stairs by their nurse, Marie.

The duke stepped forward and without a word led the little boys toward the front door. At that moment, Louis, realizing something was wrong, broke free. He hadn't said good-bye to his mama. He ran to her, sobbing. Hugo too, anchored himself to his mother's waist.

"I want to stay, Papa, please let me stay," said Hugo. "I will look after *Maman*."

The duchess, her eyes filled with tears, did her best to reassure the boys that all was well. Still they clung to her, knowing it wasn't.

Didier shrugged his shoulders and looked at Yann as if to say, "Now what?"

Yann knelt in front of little Louis and turned the small tear-streaked face to his.

"You know you must be quiet," he said gently. Louis nodded and, fixated by those deep dark eyes, stopped his crying. A sleepy calmness overcame him.

"You know you must be brave," continued Yann.

Louis nodded and put his thumb in his mouth, letting go of the folds of his mother's pale blue, watered-silk dress, his small handprint like a treasure shadowed there. He leaned his head on Yann's shoulder. Yann lifted him and handed him to Didier.

Then he knelt again and, cradling Hugo's face in his hand, stopped his crying. Didier carried them both out of the hall and down the stone steps to the waiting horses.

The duchess watched, tears running down her face. She handed Yann a long thin rag of patchwork.

"Louis is fond of it," she said. "Thank you."

Yann descended the steps two at a time, mounted his horse, took hold of the reins, and checked that all was as it should be. Didier had Hugo in front of him, just as the duke had little Louis.

They set off at a gallop. Only at the gates did the duke glance back at the château and say, "How did it come to this?"

Last night's storm had brought down branches, filling the roads with debris. For safety's sake they went by untrodden paths beside furrowed fields and stagnant streams, through empty forests, the horses' hooves sounding like a drumbeat as they galloped over the moor where the sky was vaster than the land. Yann stood in his stirrups and breathed in, feeling at one with his horse, relishing life.

I have seen too much of death. I have seen too many good men defeated at the guillotine. And what has been gained by such senseless waste? If the tree of liberty grows out of bloodshed, what rotten fruit will it bear?

Sido is like me, he thought. Why have I doubted her?

She is my strength, not my weakness. She is my desire. We are bound by the golden threads of light.

Ahead lay a dense wall of fog. It rolled in off the sea, taking with it all the surrounding scenery, swallowing up the horizon. Hidden somewhere in its folds was the faint sound of waves rushing in over the pebbled shore.

"This is as far as we go," said Yann.

The duke looked worried as he dismounted. Holding Louis tight, he shouted, "There's no way down the cliff here. It's an almost sheer rock face."

Yann took no notice of him. Instead he gathered the reins and walked the horses a little way off.

"I tell you . . ." The duke trailed off.

He was watching Yann whispering to the horses before letting them go. "I thought Gypsies were the only people on God's earth who could talk to their animals like that."

"So I've been told," said Yann.

He went over to Didier. "I think we might find a reception party waiting for us down there."

Didier took out his pistol. Yann nodded. "We'd better hope the boatman hasn't left." He looked back at the duke. "Are you ready?"

Yann went first, edging his way along a narrow path

at the top of the cliff, and then dropping into a crevice. There, hacked out of the rock, well hidden from view, was a flight of precarious stone steps leading to the pebble beach.

"It was a smugglers' cove, I believe," said Didier. "Still is, more than likely."

They could hear the roar of the sea close by. Out of sight, hidden in the pocket of fog, the tide had begun to turn. It wouldn't be long before the cove was underwater and all hope of rescue gone.

Suddenly they heard voices.

"Soldiers?" whispered Didier.

"Yes," replied Yann. "Half a dozen, I think. No doubt waiting for the butcher, to make sure they're not swindled out of their money."

"Where do you think they are?" asked Didier.

"Hard to tell, but we must find the boatman before he's forced to leave."

They set off along the beach. Even the sound of the foaming waves failed to mask the noise of their feet ringing loud like bells on a Sunday.

"Halt! Who goes there?" shouted a disembodied voice.

"It's Sergeant Berigot. Is that you, Citizen Loup?"

"That's right," growled Yann as Didier continued

down to the sea, relieved to see their boatman rowing with difficulty toward the beach. He waded into the sea to greet the sailor. Holding the prow of the boat, like Gulliver, he hauled it toward the shore as if it were a child's plaything. Then he carefully put Hugo in it.

The boy sat quietly. He seemed in a trance.

"Have you got Tull with you?" shouted the sergeant from the beach.

Tull, thought Yann, shocked. That old rogue is in on this. He called out, "Yes. Where are you?"

"Over here. Where are the goods? Have you got them down on the beach? My men are waiting to help."

The duke, certain he was about to be arrested, pushed past Yann and began wading toward Didier and the boat.

"Tull, where are you?" Out of the white fog a blue-coated soldier appeared, pistol at the ready. He stared at Yann, amazed. "Who the blazes are you?"

Yann's answer was to rush at him. The pistol went off. The duke, turning to see who was firing, lost his footing. He and Louis disappeared beneath the waves. Just as Didier let go of the boat to try to save them, the duke emerged spluttering from the water.

"Louis has gone! I had him in my arms and then—"

By now Yann had another Bluecoat down on the pebbles. Sitting astride him he knocked him unconscious. In the distance came the sound of more feet crunching along the beach toward them. Yann stood up, tore off his coat, and ran into the sea.

"Get out of the water, Didier! You can't swim—the weight of your coat will pull you under. Just keep these soldiers off me."

Didier did as he was told and waded toward the shore, pulling a knife.

"Get into the boat!" Yann shouted to the duke.

Hugo had woken from his trance. He was standing in the boat crying, while the sailor tried his best to stop it from capsizing.

Yann dived. Instantly the freezing water blinded him. He could feel his skin shrink on his head, the coldness of the water snatching his breath. He came up, then went down again, everything so dark, time running out. His mind whirled.

Don't use your eyes. Your eyes can't be trusted. The words of Tobias the Gypsy came to him in the misery of the icy water.

He could sense the child being buffeted one way

and another by the strong current that was slowly but surely sucking him out to sea. Yann grabbed the threads of light. They were losing their living zig-zag quality. He knew the child's life was ebbing. He pulled as hard as he could, coming up for air again as he did so.

Didier was still battling with the soldiers when the fog cleared sufficiently for them to be distracted by the sight of a child emerging from the sea, as if being reeled in on a giant's fishing line. It was the last image the soldiers saw, for in that moment Didier delivered his final blows.

Yann climbed into the boat, lifting Louis up and instinctively breathing into him.

"Oh Lord," wept the duke, "is he dead?"

Gradually Yann felt life coming back to the child. Louis began choking and spluttering.

"Quick, a blanket!" he ordered the sailor, and wrapping Louis up tight, gave him to the duke. Then he climbed out of the boat into the sea.

"When you arrive in Brighton, ask for Mr. Laxton."

"I owe you my life, sir," said the duke, "and that of my son. God bless you."

Yann waded back to shore and, picking up his coat,

draped it over his soaking clothes; he watched the boat disappear into the fog.

Didier looked at the prostrate bodies of the sergeant and his men, all knocked out cold, sprawled on the shingle like flotsam and jetsam.

"I wish we could leave silver blades pinned like medals to their coats."

"Come on, Didier."

"Don't you think they deserve them?"

"I think I should never have done such a foolish thing in the first place."

"Why not?"

"Because it could easily have given us away. Anyway, Têtu has forbidden it."

Didier sighed. "That's another story."

Yann didn't reply. He walked wearily toward the cliff steps. Both of them were soaking wet and shivering, water squelching in their shoes. Up on the cliff top Yann whistled for the horses.

Didier mounted and rode off, imagining Sergeant Berigot's face when he came to.

Yann sat for a moment in his saddle looking over the Channel toward the English coast and asked the wind how long it would be until he saw Sido again.

Chapter Six

A notice had been posted at the front of the theater of the Circus of Follies. It read: By order of the Committee of Public Safety the show *The Harlequinade* will reopen tonight.

The whole company knew exactly what that meant and how much danger they were all in, for Yann and Didier had not returned from Normandy. And without Mr. Margoza, there was no Harlequin. Basco, the Italian fencing teacher, was at his wits' end, and he had good reason to be. Since the success of *The Harlequinade*, Citizen Aulard had let it be known that the star of the show was Aldo Basco, the great Italian clown from Naples.

"But I am a fencing master from Sicily," Basco protested.

"It doesn't matter," said Citizen Aulard firmly, "that's our little secret."

"What if I have to act?"

Heaven help us if that day arrives, Citizen Aulard thought, but said, "Don't worry; as long as we keep Yann's true identity from the authorities, all will be well."

These were the days of conscription when young Frenchmen like Yann were expected to fight for their country. The trouble was that although Basco looked the part, he had been completely honest when he said he could not act his way out of a paper hat. Now, with less than an hour before the curtain was due to rise, the poor man was feeling sick to his stomach. Clutching his rosary, he prayed with all his might that the Virgin Mary and any other saint of wayward and lost travelers would hear his prayer and bring Yann back in time, before they were all sent to the tribunal and the death carts.

Upstairs in his office, Citizen Aulard paced back and forth, his nails chewed to the quick, while Têtu sat on the edge of a chair, Iago the parrot perched on the back.

"I suppose Basco could come in on crutches and limp through his part. After all, the theater has been closed for five days on account of his supposed sprained ankle. *Mort bleu*, I wish now I'd said he'd broken a leg."

"It would have made little difference," said Têtu, looking sadly at his friend. "We would still have been ordered to put on a show."

"Five days I've been rehearsing Basco," said Citizen Aulard, who looked tired, "and there has been no improvement, none. He's a wooden doll, a puppet. What are we going to do?"

"I'll work the magic," said Têtu, "and make it look as if he's performing Yann's tricks." He got out of his chair. "I'm teaching Yann a new one."

"What's that?"

Têtu handed Citizen Aulard a piece of paper.

"Where did you get this from?" asked the theater manager.

"Get what, my friend?"

"Why, this bill! Who spent this money?"

"Look again."

Citizen Aulard stared in amazement. Nothing. Just a plain piece of paper.

"Why, that's marvelous. Quite extraordinary!"

"Then I will do the magic tonight."

"It's not the magic that worries me," said Citizen Aulard. "He'll give the game away the minute he appears on stage." He threw up his arms and exclaimed, "We are lost. What will become of Iago?"

Much had changed since the days when Citizen Aulard had managed the Theater of Liberty in the rue du Temple, and one of the main transformations started with the theater manager himself. He had become passionate about the real-life drama that was happening outside his proscenium arch; the appalling tragedies played out daily, seasoned as always with the pepper of pathos, in the courtrooms of the tribunal.

The injustice of it all had struck Citizen Aulard like a bolt of lightning, for what is liberty—what does liberty stand for if it is not the right to free will? The right to free speech? The right to come and go as one pleases? More important still, what did it say about the leaders of the Revolution if they cared so little for their fellow men that they argued there was virtue in terror? Surely that way lies the end of the world?

Têtu agreed wholeheartedly with his sentiments.

"Fine words are what all actors want," he replied, "but only the few and the brave are called upon to act."

To Têtu's astonishment Citizen Aulard had acted, and Têtu had been genuinely moved by this newly courageous man, a sheep in borrowed lion's clothes, who was determined to play his part helping citizens escape, even if it cost him his life.

Yann, Têtu, and Citizen Aulard had set about gathering a small company of trusted actors, an eccentric menagerie of misfits. Every one of them had his or her reasons for joining such a dangerous venture; all of them knew their lives were at stake if it failed.

The decision to move to new premises had arisen due to Citizen Aulard's realization that the theater on the rue du Temple was too open to prying eyes. After all, this was the age of spies, of busybodies and nosy neighbors, of flapping ears and loose tongues. There was no choice but to find another venue with easier access to the road to the coast.

The Circus of Follies, as it was known, was on the south bank of the Seine situated in a muddle of streets off the rue Jacob, hidden in an undistinguished square. There, squashed in between the crowded tenement blocks with a few wretched shops and one grubby café to keep it company, it looked ill at ease with its surroundings, desperately waiting to be found.

And Yann had found it, not from above but from below in the catacombs, while he was trying to find a way out of Paris that bypassed the barricades and gates. Down in those ancient Roman limestone quarries, long since abandoned, was a honeycomb of tunnels and caves and passages. This is where Yann began his search.

In between shows, he would disappear for days, carrying with him enough supplies to last up to a week. On these journeys he started mapping the routes, helped by work carried out before the Revolution, when the catacombs had been reinforced to stop Paris from subsiding into the abyss. The workers, afraid, Yann supposed—as he was himself—of getting lost, had written on the walls the names of the corresponding streets above.

To begin with, Yann was disorientated by the darkness, a sensation he wasn't used to, for the dark had never bothered him. Yet here, where no sunlight had ever been, the darkness had an altogether unfamiliar texture. No dawn would break through these shadowy corridors. This darkness would never remember the light of a lantern; it would be nothing more than a pinprick in the liquid heart of eternal night. So powerful was this absence of light that for the first time, Yann experienced the sensation of being blind.

After a while, he began to find in this strange subterranean world a place of peace where he could think, without the lights and noise of Paris to distract him.

Over the weeks, he refined what he needed to take with him. A hammock was essential, so when exhaustion played havoc with his sense of direction he could restore it by sleeping.

The beauty—the underground streams, the cavernous chambers, the mysterious writing on the walls—began to work a magic on him. The discovery of an abandoned shoe touched him deeply. A memento weighted with all the desire for life, made more poignant still by the bones brought from Paris graveyards and arranged along the walls.

It was one day, one night—he didn't know—after many hours of exploring when Yann finally stopped, knocked some nails into the walls, and climbed into his hammock. He was drifting off to sleep in a twilight between dreams and reality when he thought he heard a whispering.

"Damask and death,
Velvet and violence."

The Sisters Macabre were singing to him.

He was out of his hammock in a flash. Lighting his lantern, he lifted it high and looked behind and in front. Nothing, just a long passage that disappeared into blackness. Was it a dream? They had appeared to him before in nightmares, the Seven Sisters Macabre, the tragic automata Kalliovski had created from the corpses of his most beautiful victims.

"Calico and corpses,
Taffeta and torture."

By the light of his lantern Yann saw a passage hewn out halfway up the wall. He knew now that he was awake. He crawled into the dank space, pushing his knapsack ahead of him. He emerged in a high-ceilinged room. It was empty. Shining the lantern he looked up and realized he was staring into a shaft: an escape route. Yann took out his map. He had found many such escape routes, but for various reasons none were usable. They were too exposed or just plain unsafe. He needed one that came up into the city out of sight. Carefully he clambered to the top of the shaft where an old, rickety spiral staircase protruded into the void, and cautiously started to climb, uncertain if it would collapse under his weight.

It was sturdier than he had thought and he found himself in a cellar. At one end was a narrow wooden door that needed all his strength to open. It led into a derelict building that was home to hundreds of startled pigeons.

As far as he could make out it was a small playhouse that looked as if it was about to come tumbling down.

The next day Citizen Aulard made inquiries into who owned the building, and with the financial backing of Charles Cordell and Henry Laxton, he bought the rundown theater.

Citizen Aulard oversaw its restoration, organizing carpenters and scene painters to repair the stage and generally make the place more appealing. On opening night, the show, a pantomime, went well. Magic was what nearly all the citizens of Paris hungered for—anything to escape what was happening day by day. Those faithful few in the audience who could remember Topolain and his talking Pierrot were in agreement that Basco's Harlequin outshone even the great magician.

With a stage full of actors, and many changes of scenery, there was so much to distract the eye that one hardly noticed there were extra players on some nights: a portly clown, or Colombine's charming maid, or two butcher boys, who were in reality a merchant and his family in disguise, waiting to be taken to the catacombs and then out of Paris and to the coast.

Now there were fewer than twenty minutes to the

moment when the drums would begin to roll and the curtain would rise on a terrified Basco.

Citizeness Manou, who guarded the stage door, entered the theater manager's office. She was an unprepossessing sight, with the pipe she had taken to smoking attached to her bottom lip, wrapping her in a fog of wispy smoke in which she wheezed and puffed continuously.

"Are they back?" said Têtu, spinning around.

"No," she puffed. "Here, this came for Yann." She handed Têtu a letter. "Thought it might be important."

"No sign of him? Nothing, nothing at all?" asked Citizen Aulard.

"No, unless he has become invisible. Nothing would get past me. Just the letter." She left, her shoes echoing loudly on the wooden stairs.

"That's another thing," said Citizen Aulard. "These letters. If they fell into the wrong hands, you know what that would mean."

"Death," said Têtu helpfully.

"*Mort bleu*, as if we didn't have enough to worry about. I thought you'd spoken to Yann. No good will come of this infatuation. The world may have gone insane, but it still clings tightly to its prejudices."

They were interrupted again, this time by Harlequin's leading lady, Colombine, dressed in full costume and holding her mask.

"Are we going on stage or not?" she demanded. "The cast are downstairs and they don't know what's happening. Is there any news of Yann?"

Colombine was a pretty girl with a sharp, foxy face. She could have been a fine actress if she had not been so in love with herself, and with making sure that everyone in the company felt the same way about her. Only one person had not succumbed to her charms, and that was Yann. But nothing attracted her more than a man who refused to see what she had to offer.

"I mean, I can't do this show single-handed, and I can't act with a lump of wood."

Basco entered dressed as Harlequin, looking as if he were about to go to the guillotine.

Colombine sighed. "Give me strength." Putting her hands on her hips, she said, "Well, it looks like we'll all be laying down our lives if Yann don't show up."

Tears had started to fall down Harlequin's cheeks. Citizen Aulard handed him his handkerchief as once more the door opened.

"What?" shouted Citizen Aulard. "Does no one

knock in this building? Is my room just a thorough-fare?"

"Sorry, chief," said Pantalon, one of the oldest members of the company, an actor who would have retired if it were not for the fact that most young men were in the army.

"It's a full house, chief. I'm pretty sure I saw Robespierre in the audience. I mean, this isn't going well, is it?"

"No!" shouted Citizen Aulard.

"That's what we were thinking. I was wondering if running away and hiding might be the answer."

"No," said Têtu.

"Thought as much," said Pantalon.

He looked at Basco. "Oh, no, chief, you ain't really going to put him on stage?"

"*Vive la Révolution!*"

Everyone jumped to attention. Everyone except Têtu.

"Iago, not now," said Citizen Aulard, looking angrily at the parrot. "I'd like to know whose little joke it was to teach my parrot that."

There was silence.

"Well, that's that then," said Pantalon. "I mean, we are in for it."

"Oh, get out, the lot of you," said Citizen Aulard, "and Basco, pull yourself together. Curtain up in ten minutes."

Once the actors had gone Citizen Aulard sat down with a bump in his chair.

"Vive la Révolution!"

"Mort bleu! Mort bleu!" said Citizen Aulard, leaping to his feet again. "Will you stop saying that!" He threw a book at the parrot, who flew to sit on Têtu's head in indignation.

"My friend," said Têtu. "Best we keep our nerve. All is not lost."

"Not quite. In ten minutes, yes."

The musicians started to play, the actors took their places. The curtain rose, the drums rolled, cueing Harlequin's entrance.

"Remember," said Têtu to Basco, "stay where I can see you."

Basco had sweat pouring off him and was looking wobbly.

"No, no, no, you don't faint in my theater," said Citizen Aulard, snapping his fingers in Basco's face. "That isn't allowed."

Basco bent his head, his hands on his knees, his face pea green. The drums rolled again for Harlequin to enter.

"I can't," moaned Basco. "I can't do it. Forgive me. Anything but this. Death is preferable."

"And death it will be for all of us if you don't get your backside on that stage!" shouted Citizen Aulard.

The audience, sensing something was wrong, began clapping and whistling and shouting for Harlequin. Citizen Aulard was about to stop the show when a large hand grabbed him from behind.

"No need to worry, guv," a familiar voice said. "It's covered."

Têtu and Citizen Aulard spun around, openmouthed, to see Didier standing there and beside him, Yann, already dressed as Harlequin.

"Sorry, it took longer than we thought," said Didier, as Yann, putting on his mask, made his entrance to howls of delight.

Chapter Seven

Later, after the show, Yann sat in his dressing room among the clutter of clothes, wigs, and makeup. He was exhausted. Didier, unlike him, had been able to go straight to bed. Yann had had to keep going. He was dozing when he was woken by Citizen Aulard and Têtu, Iago perched on the dwarf's shoulder.

"That was very close. Too close," said Citizen Aulard. "Basco nearly had a heart attack and as for Iago, he thought he was meat for *coq au vin*. What went wrong?"

"The weather, the road, not taking horses, not having enough safe houses. Shall I continue?" Yann sighed. "Please, I'm tired. Can we talk about this tomorrow?"

Citizen Aulard patted him on the shoulder. "Of course," he said, turning to leave. He glanced back into the dressing room to see the dwarf sitting close to Yann and, not for the first time, felt like a foreigner in their private world.

Têtu waited for the door to close, waited for Yann to take off his makeup, waited until he had changed back into his clothes. When he had waited long enough, he took from his coat a bottle of wine, cheese, bread and boiled eggs, an apple, some nuts, and two slices of cake.

Yann couldn't help but smile, remembering how, when he was little, it was one of Têtu's great tricks to conjure food from thin air.

Finally, he produced two glasses and a knife.

"You must be hungry." Têtu spoke in Romany. It was Yann's mother tongue, the language they always spoke when they were alone together, the language of their souls.

Yann laughed. "Têtu, I'm pleased to see you."

"The same."

"I thought you didn't like that parrot," said Yann. Iago was perched now, like some exotic hat, on the dwarf's head.

"He has a very good nature and I had overlooked the fact that he is a remarkably wise bird."

Iago, as if on cue, flew to sit on top of the mirror, a

better vantage point from which to observe the conversation.

"Well, what on earth delayed you for so long?"

"Vive la Révolution!" squawked the parrot.

Têtu shrugged. "I've started to teach him a few useful words," he said by way of explanation.

Yann tipped back his chair and laughed.

"What really happened?" asked Têtu.

"The weather," said Yann, his face serious, "an attempted burglary at the château, and a butcher having a heart attack."

Têtu listened carefully to all Yann had to say—and all he didn't mention.

"Mr. Tull is involved in the business of exporting stolen furniture to England, a very profitable little industry apparently."

"Did you see him?"

"No," said Yann, running his hands through his thick black hair. "There's no doubt it's getting harder to get people out. The National Guard is on the alert. They seem to be everywhere, and people are so frightened, they're willing to sell their grandmothers, or anything else they might own, to avoid being arrested."

"I believe it will get worse," replied Têtu. His face was

grave. "Yannick," he asked, "do you have your talisman?"

"How do you know about that?" asked Yann, wondering why he was ever surprised by all Têtu knew.

"Because I saw it around your neck a long time ago and I realize I have been fooling myself, imagining that you still have it."

"I gave it to Sido," said Yann. "She needs it more than I do."

Têtu got off his chair and started to walk up and down the dressing room.

"Stop it, Têtu," said Yann. "It is up to me what I do with it."

Têtu looked worried, more worried than Yann thought the situation demanded, and for a moment he felt a jolt as if he had missed something, though what, he wasn't sure.

"Tobias Cooper gave you the talisman."

"Yes, how do you know that?"

"It is irrelevant, it is nothing. I know. It is the bora bora, the shell of the shells. The emblem of light, a charm against evil, an agent of great luck—and you gave it away?"

"I didn't give it away to *anyone*. I gave it to Sido. That makes all the difference."

"You gave it to someone who is not of our blood, who will no doubt discard it as a trifle, a pretty bauble to be lost."

"No," said Yann, "you don't know her. I do, and I know she would never let it go."

"Yann, you need it. *You* are the one in danger, not Sido. It will protect you from the darkness."

"Then she and the shell are my talismans. They will bring me good luck. Together they make me even stronger."

Têtu sat down and let out a sigh. "So much is wasted on the young," he said. "This will only break your heart. . . . My advice is to get the shell back and try to forget all about her."

"No, Têtu, that is not how it is. With deep respect, this is nothing to do with you."

"Do you think for a moment that the Laxtons would be glad to know of your feelings for her?"

"I don't know," said Yann. "That is between Sido and me."

"What's between you? Some letters and the sea. Yann, this will never work! The Laxtons may hold radical views, but do you think they would relish the idea of their long-lost niece marrying a Gypsy? She may not have a dowry, but I tell you this, she has a title that is over five hundred years old and that in itself is worth a fortune."

"You're wrong," he said, knowing full well that Têtu's reasoning was sound. "The Laxtons treated me like a son."

"You're blind!" said Têtu. "Can't you see this is madness? This is their niece we are talking about."

"I love her," said Yann flatly. "What does anything else matter?"

"Yannick, let it go, I beg of you! Find another girl, someone who is—"

"What, Têtu?" said Yann angrily. "Someone who is . . . more of my class, more of my breeding?"

"Yes, a Gypsy, why not?"

"Tell me about when you met my mother."

"No, Yannick, no."

"Yes, it is the same. You have always loved Anis. Do you think I don't know that? Why didn't you find someone else when she died?"

"It's different," said Têtu, for once at a loss as to what to say.

"I don't believe that, neither do you. I am like you, Têtu, we were made to love only once. Even if I can never be with Sido, I will love no one else."

Both were silent. Words hung between them. Yann had learned how to hide his thoughts from Têtu. He could feel the dwarf's frustration.

"You are your own man. I must let it go, I see that," said Têtu. He rose to leave.

"Wait," said Yann. "There is something. That first day of the September Massacre—when Kalliovski was torn to pieces by the mob."

"Yes."

"You said something that I have been thinking about a lot lately. You said that day the devil went walking, looking for one irredeemable soul to blow his fiery life into."

Têtu nodded. "It's an old Gypsy tale."

"Do you think he did go walking?"

"I don't know," said Têtu, sitting down again.

"There is a story on the streets," replied Yann.

"Which one? You hear all sorts of tales in the cafés of Paris. Shall I tell you one I hear quite often? About a corrupt corporal who found a silver blade from a toy guillotine hanging over his head? Shall I carry on?"

"No," said Yann, refusing to catch his eye.

"I hope you are never stupid enough to do that again."

"I told you it was a joke, nothing more. I thought he would keep quiet."

"Hmm. In my bitter experience, corrupt corporals tend never to keep quiet. The name has stuck like mud, and the odd thing is that every time someone escapes and no one can work out the rhyme or reason of it, they say it is the Silver Blade."

"So I've heard. No, the story I'm talking about is the mysterious figure who is seen with his black dog in the Place de la Révolution. Some say he is real, others that he is a ghost. Some say he is the spirit of the Terror. Have you heard this story?"

"Yes," Têtu said. His face remained motionless. What could he tell Yann? That he lived in dread of Kalliovski's resurrection and the power that would come with it?

"Didier was sure we were followed from Paris by a wolf," said Yann. "I saw its shadow. I felt it belonged to the darkness."

"Why?"

"There were no threads of light. It made me wonder: If the devil went walking, and took Kalliovski, what would have happened to Balthazar?"

"A good question. One I need to think about." Têtu

moved toward the door. He clicked his fingers, and Iago flew and landed once more on his shoulder.

"One other thing," said Yann. "I heard Anis's voice. I'm sure she was warning me."

Têtu said nothing. He wanted this conversation to be over. It brought back memories of Anis. Her loss was a hole in his heart that time had forgotten to mend.

He said, more briskly than he meant to, "You need your talisman. Good night."

Yann watched him leave and then turned to the mirror, where he saw propped against it a letter from Sido.

He broke the seal and read:

Those simple words "I love you" are the most precious gems I have ever been given. I have not dared to believe that you could care for me or that your feelings could match mine. I felt it would be my secret, that I would never have the courage to tell you that I loved you with all my being.

When I arrived in London all those months ago I had never experienced a loss quite like that of being parted from you. Only in your shell did I find comfort. I would lay it on the palm of my hand and see it almost shimmer as I asked it if you were safe. It has a voice, soft, like a gentle wave lapping at the seashore; it always sings the same song: "He must love you so much to have given away such a talisman, he must love you so much . . ." A lullaby to soothe my troubled heart.

What would I have done without your letters? Don't think I don't know what danger they put you in, but I have counted the days between them, been frustrated beyond belief when there wasn't anything from you, and even my dear postman would look sad. Poor Mr. Trippen, I think if he could have conjured a letter from thin air, he would have done so.

There is no one else. Goodness knows what you have heard. It is true that my uncle and aunt have introduced me into society. I can tell you this: All I ever meet is empty-headed or vain young men. I feel like an automaton dressed up and wheeled out. My fault, I fear, for once again I have retreated into silence. There are no words I want to share with anyone but you.

Here my soul is imprisoned. Only you can set it free.

You have been with me in everything. And you will always be with me. You are my beginning; you will be my end; in the middle lies our future. I am with you in spirit, as I feel your spirit is with me. I will wait, Yann. You and only you have the key to my soul.

Je t'aime.

Sido

Chapter Eight

When Sido arrived eighteen months earlier, she found London a noisy old lady wheezing monstrous in all her smoke and fumes. With her mantle of twisting narrow streets oozing into the countryside, uncontained by city walls, she was so different from Paris that to begin with, Sido felt bewildered.

She was further bewildered by her aunt and uncle's genuine love of her. Juliette had tears in her eyes when Sido first entered the drawing room in Queen Square for, as she told her, she looked almost identical to the beloved sister she had lost.

That was their only similarity, as Juliette soon discovered, for here was a young woman who possessed not only beauty but understanding that exceeded her years. In her aunt's eyes, Sido's gentleness made the cruelty of what she had suffered even more repugnant. The Laxtons felt very protective of her. There was a vulnerability about Sido that Juliette thought came from neglect. Henry knew it had more to do with the atrocities she had witnessed in the Abbaye prison and the ordeal she had suffered at the hands of Kalliovski. He shuddered to think of the obscene marriage contract and what would have happened if Yann hadn't rescued her.

It had been Mr. Trippen, Yann's old tutor, who, sensing Sido's feelings toward his former pupil, had encouraged her to write to him. That first letter had taken ages, and when it was finally finished she felt it was stiff, awkward, and childish. Her only hope was that Yann might see all the invisible words written between the lines, words her quill was too shy to shape. She had left it on the silver plate in the hall with all the other letters to be posted.

That afternoon Juliette and Sido sat in the drawing room, Juliette at her needlework, Sido reading, as the fire crackled in the grate and the clocks ticked gently.

Outside, horses clip-clopped by and Sido, half dreaming, did not at first hear her aunt when she said,

"My dear, I hope you don't mind, but I took the liberty of removing the letter from the hall table."

Sido was suddenly wide-awake.

"Here it is," said Juliette, handing it back to her. "Please don't think me rude, but it is really not safe to write to Yann."

"I wanted to thank him," said Sido, feeling her cheeks flame.

"My goodness," said Juliette, "it is a very good thing you didn't. If he were to receive a letter from an émigré, it could be used in evidence as proof that he was a counterrevolutionary or a spy. Isn't that dreadful?" She paused. "Anyway, your uncle tells me that his role as Harlequin attracts quite enough letters from ardent young ladies."

The very idea that she would be just one of Yann's many doting admirers appalled Sido. Mortified, she said, "It is only that I have known him for some time."

Juliette smiled. "Of course, *ma cherie*. He must seem like a hero to you. But believe me when I say he would understand. I'm sure there are many young women in Paris bewitched by those dark eyes of his, don't you think?"

Sido wished the floor would open and swallow her

whole. Was she another silly little girl, infatuated by a young man who had taken the liberty of stealing her heart and kissing her for it? She put the letter in the fire, watching it burn.

"It is for the best," said her aunt.

———

Sido's spirits over that first long, dull winter in London had been very low indeed. She did all that was required of her, but with little enthusiasm. She felt dead inside. A terrible melancholy hung over her like a London fog that nothing could lift. She was haunted by nightmares of Kalliovski, of his beetle-black carriage.

In these dreams she knows she is to be the count's bride. She is in a huge domed chamber in which stands a macabre altar made from the dismembered bodies of the victims of the Abbaye massacre, their limbs protruding, their hands moving, their fingers twitching, blood dripping onto the floor. In front of the altar stand seven women, screaming through sewn-up lips:

"Calico and corpses.

Damask and death."

Kalliovski turns his waxen face to Sido, his red lips a wound. "Don't let the blood stain your white, white dress, my dear."

Every time, she would wake, terrified, shaking, and light all the candles in the room.

Often she wouldn't sleep for fear of the nightmare. On those nights, she would sit looking into the fire, her knees pulled up under her chin, her arms wrapped around her legs and think, what if she never saw Yann again? What then was the point to living? So much had happened since the time she had first woken to see him standing by her bed. The only consistent thing in her life, which had never failed her, was Yann. No one in London understood her. She was treated like a china doll, to be worshipped like a goddess, as one handsome dandy had told her. The thought made her shudder.

Concerned for her health, Juliette and Henry sought advice from the best doctors in London. All agreed that news of what was happening in France was to be kept to a minimum. Henry believed this to be balderdash. Sido possessed far too lively a mind to be unaware of events in Paris, and it would be near impossible to spare her from such conversations, as they had an open house for émigrés three times a week. At these gatherings Sido's spirits would perceptibly rise, especially when the Silver Blade was mentioned, as if instinctively she knew who they were talking about.

Henry's diagnosis was altogether more astute. The real reason for Sido's unhappiness was her longing for Yann, but on that subject it was impossible to speak. It had been Yann's decision that Juliette should not be told the truth about what he did. Juliette had been devoted to him, and if she thought that he hadn't run away to be an actor, but was dancing with death, playing a dangerous role in the Revolution, she would have driven herself to distraction with worry. Henry agreed it was far better that she was allowed to think Yann was an ungrateful young man who had given up a golden opportunity to go to Cambridge.

Not for the first time, he was considering the wisdom of his decision. It was as clear as day, whether they liked it or not, his earnest and very beautiful young niece was in love with Yann Margoza.

It was in the new year, at one of their English lessons, that Mr. Trippen handed Sido a letter. Her surprise at seeing her name written on it nearly took her breath away.

"Do you know who it's from, my dear young lady?" asked Mr. Trippen.

Sido felt her heart beat faster and her words freeze on her tongue.

"I believe the handwriting, if my eyes don't deceive me, is that of a young Hamlet," said Mr. Trippen.

"By Hamlet, you mean Yann?"

"I do indeed. Mr. Margoza wrote to me to ask if I would make sure this was personally delivered to you here. He feels Mr. and Mrs. Laxton might not think it proper or wise for you to correspond with him. He also wrote that if you agree with them, then he won't write again."

The expression that crossed Sido's face told Mr. Trippen all he needed to know. Sido was in love with Yann, and he with her. Just as he had suspected.

"If you're worried about the safety of sending such a letter, all I need tell you is that Mr. Margoza has arranged the whole thing. My task is by far the more pleasurable: to make sure it gets into your fair hand."

"Thank you," said Sido, and she smiled. "I have never written a letter before. I tried and it sounded so stiff. Anyway, it ended in the fire."

"Now, as for the writing of letters, one has to make a start. To that end, there is always the 'Dear So-and-So' to rely on, but once that is said, an acre of white paper can be most off-putting."

"That is where I was having trouble."

"Be brave, as the great bard would say. Nothing can come of nothing. No good worrying too much about politeness and etiquette. My advice is to speak what's in your heart. Be yourself."

So started the secret exchange of letters that made London bearable for Sido, made cloudy skies sunny, and gave her the greatest happiness she had ever known. They wrote of everything and nothing; with each letter they ventured deeper, like two people wading out to sea, hoping when the time came they would know how to swim. After more than twelve months of correspondence, Yann had finally written to tell her he loved her.

In April 1794, Sido first saw the strange man. It happened after she had been at the Trippens'. She had arrived to find the whole household in nothing short of uproar, and Mrs. Trippen in a terrible state.

"Mice is what's done it," said Mrs. Trippen, standing on a chair while her daughters were similarly arranged around the breakfast room, leaving the son and heir to try to catch the little thing.

"My dear enchanting girl," she cried, "we are waiting for Mr. Trippen to return with the cat who resides on Drury Lane, known for its expertise with mice. In the meantime I suggest that you climb onto the table."

Sido, who had no fear of mice, went over to where the mouse in question was busily cleaning its whiskers, looking rather fat and unconcerned about humans on chairs. She remembered well the mice at the convent and one in particular she had become fond of. Bending down, she startled the creature by throwing her shawl over it and taking it outside.

Mr. Trippen then came striding in. "I have Mr. Tibbets!" he cried with gusto. The cat, a ginger tom, looked a vicious flea-ridden thing. Nevertheless he had a commanding presence, enough to revive Mrs. Trippen's flagging spirits.

"We are indeed at sixes and sevens," said Mr. Trippen, taking Sido upstairs. "It is unpardonable, I know, but mice are a very common problem, alas."

Sido tried her best to keep a solemn face, but was quite defeated and burst out laughing. "Oh, Mr. Trippen, it doesn't matter. I believe they even had mice at Versailles!"

"You think so?"

"Yes."

"Good," he said. "Now that I know I am on a par with royalty, I feel somewhat better."

After her lesson, Mr. Trippen saw her, as always, to the door. Two footmen waited with a sedan chair to take her back to Queen Square.

It was as she was leaving Maiden Lane that she first noticed him, a large man, his face hidden by a three-cornered hat. Although she couldn't see his features, there was something familiar about him and she had the decided impression that he was following her. She had returned home to Queen Square wondering whether to say anything to her uncle.

When she arrived, she heard her aunt calling for her and, going upstairs to the pretty first-floor drawing room, she found her sitting on a small sofa, surrounded by Yann's letters.

Sido's heart sank.

"May I ask," said her aunt, "what is the meaning of this? After you have been asked not to write to him?"

"Those are private letters," said Sido, horrified to think her aunt might have read them. "They are addressed to me."

"That is by the by." Juliette sat stiff and upright. "He

writes to you in such an informal way. Is that how you address him?"

"Aunt, you have no right—"

"I do," she interrupted. "I am your guardian. I love you, and I want what's best for you. This is folly. Yann is not an appropriate suitor for you. He has nothing—no title, no money. It would be an ill-advised and scandalous union. You have much to learn and are not acquainted with the ways of the world. This is merely a young girl's infatuation. It will pass, Sido."

"No, Aunt, it will not. I love him with all my being. I always have and I always will, no matter what. My love is steadfast. Now, may I have my letters back?" Sido asked coldly.

"You may not," said Juliette. "When Yann lived here we treated him as an equal, he was even offered a place at Cambridge. Did you know that? He could have amounted to someone. Instead he chose to squander the opportunities your uncle gave him and go back to Paris to become an actor."

"Aunt, that is not—"

"I take it that Mr. Trippen is your collaborator? He should have known better."

Sido felt the injustice of this acutely.

Her aunt's voice softened. "There are many eligible young men in London who are already in love with you. My dear one, please, this is a most inadvisable liaison, and it must stop."

Sido composed herself. "Aunt," she said, "I don't want a marriage made in a bank vault, like my mother's. I will marry for love or not at all. I refuse to live a lie like she did."

"What on earth do you mean by that?"

Sido took a deep breath. "My mother was in love with Armand de Villeduval," she said slowly. "I am their child. The marquis arranged with Count Kalliovski to have us all killed the day they tried to elope to England. Only I survived." She stopped and regarded her aunt.

Now it was Juliette's turn to be outraged. "That is not true! That can't be true! My sister would never have—"

"I know it is the truth," Sido said quietly. "I have letters and documents to prove it. Yann found them and gave them to me. The letters my mother and Armand wrote to each other prove who my real father is. I also have the note from the marquis asking the count to arrange the accident. I will not be a puppet anymore. What's in a name? And what value now does that name have? The only person who has ever loved me for who I am is Yann. He risked everything to rescue me. I would be dead if it were not for his bravery."

Furious and unable to comprehend what she had just heard, Juliette ignored it. "Can you imagine the scandal? A marquis's daughter marrying a Gypsy boy, for that is what Yann is—a Gypsy! Oh, didn't he tell you? A fine education and all he wants to do is waste his life on the stage! I refuse to let you ruin your life too."

Sido fled from the room as Henry entered.

"What on earth's going on?" he said.

Juliette was sitting as stiff as a tree before the wind bows it. Doubling over, she burst into tears.

"I demand to know the truth," she wept.

"About what?"

"Was my sister murdered?"

Henry, caught off guard, said calmly, "Who told you that?"

"Sidonie."

Henry sighed. Of course, he thought. It was inevitable.

Juliette looked up at him imploringly. "I have a right to know the truth."

"Yes," he said, going over to her and taking her hand.

"I'm afraid she was. I had my suspicions when I went to France all those years ago after the accident. At least Sido is still with us. Let the dead rest easy."

Juliette pulled her hand away and with a look of disgust said, "Why did you never tell me this? How could you keep such a thing to yourself?"

"Because you were unwell and grief-stricken, and nothing was certain, not then. Not until the papers were discovered."

"So you have seen my sister's letters?"

"Yes. But what are these letters?"

"They are love letters Yann has written to Sido," said Juliette.

"Did Sido wish you to see them?"

"No, of course not," said Juliette. "They are so . . . *forward*. They say things that shouldn't be said. Let me read you—"

"No," he said abruptly. "I will not hear them, and you, madam, should not have read them."

Never before had Juliette heard her husband address her so sternly.

"But Henry, this match—"

"Madam, you will stop interfering in matters that don't concern you."

"Sido does concern me; she's my sister's child," Juliette sobbed.

Henry went to the window. Standing below in the square was a man, his face well hidden by a three-cornered hat.

He took a deep breath to calm himself, then turned back to his wife. "When Yann came to live with us, you were in favor of taking him in as an equal, to be part of our family, remember?"

"Yes, yes, I did, and I meant it. He was, after all, a young boy. We did the right thing by him, and he let us down. We stayed true to our word."

"As long as our word suited us," said Henry bluntly.

"*Mon cheri*, surely you can see this is untenable? What kind of life would he and Sido have together? He is of inferior birth, of lowly rank. He is a Gypsy. In France, Gypsies are thought of as vermin."

Henry bristled with indignation at his wife's *petit-bourgeois* attitude. "That, to me," he said, "is the worst form of prejudice. Do you wish Sido to be like your sister, married to a man who doesn't love her? To some ridiculous handsome fop with a good eye for a horse and the indolence of too many idle years as an émigré? Being buried alive might be preferable."

"Are you determined to be unpleasant?"

"No, I'm not. But your argument can't go unchecked. Yann could well have chosen to go to Cambridge, to have taken the numerous opportunities we were more than prepared to give him, and then you would have forgotten his origins. Instead he went back to Paris and saved Sido, risked his life to get her out."

"And now he is an actor! It was his choice to stay in France."

Henry felt disappointment in Juliette. "There are things I can't discuss, and this is one of them. But you should know that Paris is more perilous than ever."

"What are you saying?"

"In a world turned upside down, we need heroes. There are not many who are prepared to risk everything. Don't you think their courage earns them the right to defy social conventions? I can assure you of this: Yann is worth a thousand foppish young men."

"But you are not listening to me. All I am saying is that he is not a suitable husband for Sido."

"You are in danger of sounding like a hypocrite, like someone who had no intention of thinking Yann an equal, who was always going to see him as a Gypsy boy.

Were you just playing a game, like Marie Antoinette pretending to be a shepherdess?"

Juliette put her head in her hands. "No, no. . . . Perhaps."

They were silent a long while.

"Give Sido back her letters," Henry said. "Make it up to her. If Yann survives . . ." He paused. "Be kind to her."

Sido's thoughts were in chaos. Yann a Gypsy! She felt suddenly foolish and ignorant. Her aunt was right. She was a child when it came to the affairs of men. Had she heard correctly? A Gypsy? And she herself was a blind fool. The talisman, his dark eyes, his ability to read her thoughts. Oh, dear Lord, this made her love for him even more impossible.

She remembered with horror the stories about the marquis's hunting parties, when he would boast that he had killed Gypsies like crows and hung them in the trees. To think that by birth she was part of a society that saw such barbarity as its God-given right!

And then she remembered a grand ball in what seemed like another lifetime, given on the day she first met Yann, the day Kalliovski had killed the magician Topolain.

She had been standing on the stairs when she overheard a young woman talking about the time the marquis had brought a fortune-teller to the house who had predicted that he would lose everything to the king of the Gypsies.

The thought lifted her spirits and, getting off the bed, she went to the window and opened the shutters. It was a cold rainy night; only a few people were out. And then, in the flare of a passing carriage lamp, she saw him again. He was looking up at her window. Sido quickly backed into the room, blowing out all the candles before she dared look once more into the square. No one was there. The stranger in the three-cornered hat had vanished.

Chapter Nine

Madame Loup said not a word when she was told her husband was dead, fearful lest she might let out a hallelujah by mistake. After all, she had prayed every day of her married life for just such a miracle as this. And slowly it dawned on her that at last she was free of the murderous thug who had as good as ruined her life.

"A tragedy. I hope they catch the aristos who've done this," said a drunk, fighting to keep his distance from the floor.

"Guillotine the lot of them!" said her neighbor Citizen Planchot, a pale fish-like creature who had always been terrified of the butcher, but felt the necessity of singing his praises now that he was dead. Madame

Loup knew all too well what the old cod was after. He was hoping he might be able to buy the business.

Madame Loup finally found her voice. "Where is Anselm?"

"No one's seen him. We can only hope he's still alive," said Citizen Planchot.

"The Spirit of the Revolution," said the drunk, hoping to be invited in for more wine, no doubt. "He'll turn up."

Like a bad penny, thought Madame Loup.

There being nothing to say, nothing to sell, and no wine she wished to share with anyone, she closed the shop for good. After that she would stand night and day by the window, studying the passersby, listening to the sign of the iron pig swinging back and forth. Neighbors believed her grief and devotion to her family kept her there, holding a vigil, waiting for Anselm to return.

But they were wrong. Very wrong indeed. She had never liked him, even as a baby. All that beauty had a stink of cruelty about it that made her sick. Anselm, as far as she was concerned, could go to hell.

Citizen Planchot came every day to report to Madame Loup on how his search for Anselm was going. He had been to taverns and gambling dens, but had neither found nor heard a thing that would give him a clue as to where the lad could be. He had even gone to the police headquarters in the Hôtel de Ville, looked in at the city prisons, and been down by the Drowned Man's Benches—slabs of stone beside the Seine where the luckless ones were fished from the river to be claimed, or not, as the case might be.

"Maybe he's been picked up and conscripted," said Citizen Planchot, hoping now his neighbor might negotiate the sale of the shop.

Still Madame Loup waited by the window, coffin-cold and unconvinced that the devil's imp was dead.

When she heard that Anselm had been seen, she knew she had no choice but to leave the shop and leave it fast. To that end, she invited Citizen Planchot around, and sitting at the kitchen table they came to an agreement. The business and the shop would be his, and Madame Loup would have enough money to return to Mallemort in Provence, her childhood home.

After he had gone, she went upstairs to her clean, sparse bedchamber and sat on the bed, sewing her new-found wealth into her best red calico petticoat. Packing a few possessions, she went back downstairs and looked around the shop for the last time. It was then she saw a figure in the gloom. Her heart sank.

He appeared, to anyone who didn't know the true color of his blood, the kind of young man to give your heart to, such were his angelic looks, those golden eyes, that sensuous mouth.

"Well, well," he said. His words snaked toward her; she could feel the venom in them.

"Sold the business, I heard. Took it into that sawdust brain of yours to do something on your own, without consulting your son and heir."

Madame Loup had been edging toward the door, but Anselm got there first.

"We can do this the civilized way," he said, "or the hard way."

"I don't know what you mean," she said. Under her red calico petticoat, her knees began to shake.

"Oh, I think you do, Mother. I want my money."

She opened her bag and showed him just a few *assignats* that she had kept back for the journey.

"You're making me angry, Mother," said Anselm quietly. "And you know what happens if you make me angry, don't you, Mother? I want all the money, every last *sou*."

Madame Loup backed away.

Anselm was in no hurry. He would get his money all right; that was not the point. The point would be the pleasure he would have in seeing her beg for mercy. He put his finger and thumb on her jaw and pushed her hard against the wall. He could feel her soft skin, tissue-thin like parchment, in his grasp.

"You'd better be careful, Mother, that you don't end up with the rotten chicken meat."

Madame Loup's face was turning blue.

"Now, I ask you again. Where's the money?"

Ever since Madame Loup had been married, she had imagined her own death as a door through which she knew escape from the final beating was possible, a place where her husband couldn't touch her. Now she worried that he might be waiting on the other side, ready to grab her. The thought was enough to make her fight with her last ounce of courage, for suddenly she knew what she wanted out of life, and that was to live without fear.

Her newfound strength excited Anselm. He liked resistance. But it was useless.

He could feel her pulse beating, knew that he only had to squeeze and the frayed thread of her life would be broken forever.

He watched emotionless as she gasped for air. Madame Loup's words were now no more than a desperate whisper; her bird-like hands had curled over, trying frantically to claw at him.

"Oh, sweet Mary, save me," she begged, with what sounded like her last breath.

Anselm had never been worried by his conscience. His moral compass, for what it was worth, his father had stolen from him long ago. The urge to kill was powerful, irrepressible inside him as he squeezed tighter. Madame Loup's eyes rolled back in her head.

All Madame Loup could see was light. It shone brightly. The Virgin Mary, she felt sure, had come to take her home.

"Leave her be," came a rough voice. "Do you hear me? I have work for you, but there'll be nothing if you kill her."

Involuntarily Anselm loosened his grip as he recognized the voice of Mr. Tull.

"Let her go," said Mr. Tull again, talking to Anselm as he would to a dog. "Let her go, you pathetic little puke-pot."

Anselm let Madame Loup drop to the floor like a pile of rags.

Realizing that she was alive and her protector, whoever he was, looked like a man strong enough to hold Anselm back, she said in a whisper, "Holy Mary, Mother of God, I tell you this, and it is the truth, you are no son of mine. I didn't bear you. You were left in a basket of stinking blood and guts. Even your real mother didn't want you. She was glad to be rid of her devil's child."

Anselm rushed toward her once more, but Mr. Tull had him by the collar.

"Save your breath to cool your porridge," Mr. Tull said.

"Go to the devil!"

As Mr. Tull dragged him from the shop, he was still screaming, "I'm going to kill her!"

Madame Loup lay on the floor for a long time, gasping for breath, until her strength returned. She sat up and drank a glass of wine. She knew she had escaped Death by a cat's whisker. It would be many years before he came calling again, walking through fields of lavender to find her.

"Well, I see the shop business ain't to your liking," said Mr. Tull, when they were seated in a café with a jug of wine in front of them. "Calm down. You're going to need your wits."

"Where've you been? I haven't seen you around for ages," said Anselm, drumming his fingers wildly on the table, his foot tapping a chaotic rhythm on the floor.

"Away on business. It seems I got back just in time."

Anselm wasn't listening. He leaped to his feet. "Let me finish her off; it's what she deserves. She owes me, she does."

"By all means," said Mr. Tull. "Go on, kill the old girl; it's no skin off my nose."

Anselm was rearranging his scarf, ready to charge back to the butcher's shop.

"The only thing is, you wouldn't get to meet Count Kalliovski."

His words had the desired effect.

"Oh," said Mr. Tull, lighting his pipe, "you're interested, then?"

"Yes."

Mr. Tull leaned forward and grabbed Anselm by the throat. "If," he said, knowing exactly where to press to cause the most pain, "you breathe a word of what you see tonight, you are a dead man and no mistake. You get my drift?"

Letting go, he poured a tumbler of wine. "Have a drink. We've got a long night ahead of us."

It was early evening when they reached the Place du Faubourg de Gloire. All that was left of the Bastille were a few stones and blackened earth.

"A place of secrets," said Mr. Tull.

"They say it's haunted by the specter of the Terror made real," said Anselm, remembering what he had been told in the whorehouse where he'd been staying.

"That wouldn't surprise me. But I think the Terror is real enough, with or without the specter."

"I've heard them say he has a big dog."

"Oh, put a rag in it."

They walked away from the Bastille, toward the Seine ferrymen who were packing up for the night.

"One last trip?" asked Mr. Tull, bringing out a good handful of coins.

"For you," said the ferryman, pushing his boat into the water, "a pleasure." He lit the lantern. "Take you to La Taverne des Trois Pendus on the other side?"

Mr. Tull nodded.

The brown water of the Seine lapped past. Until they

reached the south bank the only other sound was the swish of the oars.

They crunched up the shore and climbed the wooden steps leading to the inn.

"Is this where we're meeting him?" asked Anselm.

"No." Mr. Tull was in no mood for talking. "Sit down and shut up. I'll tell you when we need to go."

At midnight, Mr. Tull shook Anselm awake and stood him up, taking in his appearance.

"You're a mess. You don't half stink too. What, you been sleeping in the gutter?"

"No," said Anselm.

"Pull yourself together. Make yourself look respectable. One other thing. Not one word about the robberies. If you say anything, you'll be a bag of bones."

It had started to rain heavily by the time they arrived at their destination: a shop with a shuttered front. Above, in the murky window, hung three dimly lit red lanterns. The room inside was equally empty, with sawdust on the floor and a scrubbed counter on which sat a large ledger. Somewhere in the distance a bell rang. A man appeared from behind a velvet curtain. He was dressed from head to toe in black.

"Serreto," said Mr. Tull. "How are you?"

"As well as these topsy-turvy days allow." He opened the ledger in front of him and wrote something down.

Pointing his quill at Anselm he said, "He knows the rules, does he?"

Mr. Tull nodded. "He's here on probation."

"I see."

Anselm had the feeling from the look Serreto gave him that he had just been measured for a coffin.

They were taken through the curtain into an antechamber lined with row upon row of cloaks and masks. Bunches of unlit torches stood in wicker baskets, waiting to be used. Mr. Tull lit one and opened another door that led to a flight of stairs descending to the cellar—or so Anselm thought. Yet the farther they went the more he began to realize that no cellar could possibly be this deep. The stairs, made out of limestone, became narrower and spiraled, step after step, round and round. The light of Mr. Tull's torch flickered, throwing shadows across the white stone walls. And still they kept going down without end.

The air began to smell musty and damp. Finally they reached the very bottom. They were in a cavernous room that led to a tunnel, lit with torches as far as the eye could see.

"Are you ready?" said Mr. Tull.

Anselm was quiet. Mr. Tull turned to check his companion.

"A lot of people couldn't stand it down here," he said, "but you get used to it. You still with me?"

Anselm nodded, following Mr. Tull into the labyrinth of tunnels. He took a deep breath of stale air and said out loud, "This is a new beginning, and nothing is going to stop me."

"What did you say?" said Mr. Tull, turning around.

"Just that I wanted . . . I want to thank you."

"For what?"

"For giving me this opportunity. I owe you, I do."

Mr. Tull walked on. "Better hope that my master likes you."

If he doesn't, he thought, you will never see the light of day again.

Chapter Ten

Of all the châteaux Anselm and his father had robbed over the past year, nothing compared to this.

The first chamber had a higher ceiling than the passageway they had walked through. Anselm later discovered that it was only a prelude to what lay beyond—a waiting room of sorts, a place to contemplate one's own mortality.

If he had been able to read the motto above the door, he might have been more worried: *Enter here if you dare and you fear not death.* The words, no more than a pattern to Anselm, didn't interest him. What fired his imagination were the painted walls that, though he didn't know it, depicted Dante's *Inferno*. The ceiling too had been decorated so it looked as if the chandelier had been spewed out of the mouth of the devil. Three golden bowls stood near the far end of the chamber, and flames like forked tongues flickered menacingly. He was enthralled by the idea that tonight he would meet the great man himself. The master, as Mr. Tull called him.

Count Kalliovski.

Mr. Tull, unlike Anselm, seemed oblivious to his surroundings. He paced to and fro, fiddling with his watch. Seeing Anselm studying the walls he hissed at him, "Remember, not a word about our other business, understood?"

"Of course, Mr. Tull. My lips are sealed."

Mr. Tull was beginning to have his doubts about bringing Anselm here. His lack of breeding showed. He looked what he was: nothing more than a pretty boy, a small-time crook from the Place du Carrousel.

"Stop staring at everything," Mr. Tull said tartly. "Look at the floor if you're going to look anywhere."

"Why?"

"Because I say so, and because there are eyes behind them there walls."

Anselm spun around, examining everything with even more relish than before.

"Are you trying to show me up or what?" said Mr. Tull through gritted teeth. "Just stare at your bleeding shoes."

A door opened then, and into the room came a man who looked as if his skin had been patched together. He had one white fish-eye, a dead pupil staring through what looked like a film of rancid milk. His good eye, green and eager, surveyed the room. He was taller than Mr. Tull, and in the pecking order of thugs there was no doubt who was the superior. Mr. Tull seemed almost sheepish as he introduced Milkeye to Anselm.

Milkeye, ignoring the boy, said, "My master will see you now."

Anselm followed Mr. Tull. Milkeye stopped him, his hand held out like a barricade.

"Not you. You stay."

Anselm, seeing he had no alternative, waited until Milkeye returned and led him down a corridor ablaze with candles. Each was held in a skeleton hand that had been gold-leafed and decked in jewels, so that light was caught in the brilliance of the gems and reflected across the walls in radiant sparks of color. A ways off, he could hear water.

"Where's that coming from?" he asked.

"You don't speak. You don't ask questions. You do what you're told," said Milkeye, pushing open a heavy iron door for Anselm to slip through. "And now you wait until you're called for."

There was a finality, like being locked in a prison cell, to the closing of the door. For a moment Anselm was disorientated. When his eyes adjusted, he could see walls covered in a mosaic of human bones, the design punctuated by skulls, their eye sockets inlaid with a myriad mirrors, so that he was surrounded by fragments of his own mindless image. It had a giddying effect.

When a similar door at the opposite end of the room swung open—apparently of its own accord—to Anselm this was an invitation to investigate. Curiosity, the killer of cats, drove him ever onward, regardless of the words above the threshold: *The point of no return.*

The door led to a gallery beyond which he could hear voices. Slowly he slid snake-like across the wooden gantry floor toward the carved banisters. From there he looked down into a vast domed hall, its walls made from human bones stacked like logs, bare and yellowed. The ceiling blazed with a multitude of chandeliers made out of bones and lit with hundreds of candles. The floor was laid with slabs of stone, dipping slightly toward the center, where there appeared to be a small hole like a navel, stained brownish red.

Figures stood waiting, dressed in cloaks and masks. A chair hovered just off the ground, as if suspended on invisible wires.

Anselm lay welded to the spot as he heard boots click-clack across the stone floor below. A man faced the assembly, his back to the gantry. The gathering bowed deeply. He was immaculately dressed in black with red kid gloves, and wore no cloak or mask. Instinctively Anselm knew it was Count Kalliovski. The man turned and looked up as if he was aware of another's presence.

Now Anselm could see him clearly, and he shuddered as he remembered once, long ago when he was still a child, having been taken to see the waxworks in a passage off the rue St. Jacques. This man looked as if he belonged more to the waxy, embalmed dead than the living.

"I am the Terror incarnate, the engine of fear. I am your end and your beginning. Your salvation lies in my power, as does your damnation. You are my inner circle. If anyone here betrays me they will never escape my wrath."

The hall was graveyard silent.

"I, the bringer of darkness, will soon possess the power of light. That day I will rise from the ashes, a phoenix, to reign supreme."

He walked to the chair and sat down. "To the business at hand. Bring forth the Seven Sisters Macabre."

Anselm was hypnotized. Seven beautifully dressed women glided into the chamber. They were youthful and elegant, their faces hidden from him. They too bowed before Kalliovski; then one by one they began to leave the ground to be suspended in midair, just as his father had been. Slowly they spun, and now he saw why they had been given their name. They were hideous apparitions, ghastly harpies.

The chair in which Kalliovski was sitting rose higher.

"I am the master," he said.

The Seven Sisters Macabre began to chant.

"Calico and corpses."

"We have a traitor among us," Kalliovski said.

"Damask and death."

"All of you know the penalty for betrayal."

"Velvet and violence," hissed the Sisters Macabre.

"I call on Balthazar to reveal the spy in our midst."

"Brocade and blood!" Their voices reached a crescendo.

There was a rustling of fabric as the cloaked and masked figures pushed farther into the bones of the wall as if hoping to disappear.

The silence that now took hold of the chamber had a sound, just as wine has a smell. It was the high-pitched scream of terror. And then suddenly Anselm heard the howl of a beast. A shadow, liquid as molten iron, flashed past.

Anselm felt the hair rise on the back of his neck. He buried his head in his arms, imagining the great black dog was coming for him. He was certain that this was the same beast he'd seen at the Duc de Bourcy's estate, that the diabolical creature had followed him here and would smell him out.

Through screwed-up eyes he saw the beast sniff its way around the room before singling out one of the cloaked and masked figures. The poor man started to shake. His teeth chattered in fear. The hound leaped at him, pulling the mask from his face. The victim's screams were without echo, as if the walls were greedily swallowing the sound of misery. He was torn to shreds like a rag doll. The floor ran red. The beast licked it clean, then with a deep growl turned and vanished from the chamber.

Kalliovski's voice made Anselm jump.

"Those foolish enough to speak about our activities will, like Levis Artois, find their lives cut short. Anyone here who feels the necessity to discuss what is said within these walls will go the same way."

Anselm felt his insides turn to water as he was hoisted to his feet.

Milkeye said nothing as he led him away.

Kalliovski's living quarters were even more spectacular than the previous chambers. They had the luxury of windows, and Anselm almost forgot they were so far underground that there would be nothing to see. Yet through the windows were vistas of gardens, of gravel drives that looked real until he saw they had been painted. An artificial sun shone into the chamber. He even recognized some of the furniture he and Mr. Tull had taken from noble houses, now put to great effect.

As Anselm waited with Milkeye, Count Kalliovski entered the room, followed by Mr. Tull. The count's waistcoat was embroidered with silver skulls. Close up he was even more intimidating. Anselm stared, transfixed. This man acted not in the rage of the moment like his father used to. He killed in cold blood.

Count Kalliovski stood, lost in thought, his back to Anselm.

"Tell me, do you believe the Governor of the Universe created the world?"

The question was one to which Anselm had never given much thought, and he wasn't sure if he was expected to answer. He looked beseechingly at Mr. Tull, who stared resolutely at his shoes.

Kalliovski turned to look at him. "Well?"

Mr. Tull nudged Anselm.

"Yes," said Anselm uncertainly.

"I don't," replied Kalliovski. "I don't believe the Governor of the Universe had anything to do with it. It is purely by the power of chance that the world is here at all. What say you to that?"

Anselm was out of his depth. He had never been involved in this sort of conversation. If it was a test, he felt certain he was going to fail.

"All I know about religion comes from my mother, and she believes in God and all the saints. She believes in purgatory and hell." He added, more to himself than anyone else, "She thinks that's where I'm going."

"And if I told you there are no such places," asserted Count Kalliovski, "that it is the church's plot against the people, nothing more, what would you say?"

That's what Pa believed, Anselm thought. He was all for getting rid of the church. He said if the Revolution hadn't banned it, he might not have been as free with his pig-killing knife and would have worried more about what might happen to him when he was dead.

Now Anselm shrugged his shoulders. "I don't know. But if it is by chance that the world is here, as you say, then maybe there's a good chance that hell exists too?"

To Anselm's great relief Count Kalliovski's reply had a hint of laughter in it, though his face remained wax-work smooth. "You have potential," he said. "Would you like to work for me?"

"Yes," said Anselm. His puppy-like enthusiasm made Mr. Tull wince. "When do I start?"

Kalliovski glanced at him.

Anselm felt something push down on his shoulders, an invisible force. His legs gave way under the pressure and he found himself on his knees.

"You will do what I say, or you will be killed, do you understand?"

Kalliovski inclined his hand in its red kid glove, a sign that Anselm was dismissed. Milkeye helped him up and took him from the chamber, leaving only Mr. Tull.

134

From the window, the artificial glow of golden afternoon light flooded into the room, and the reassuring sound of birdsong could be heard from the cages hidden behind the painted flats.

"A nightingale," said Kalliovski.

Mr. Tull had been dreading this meeting. He had told himself repeatedly that if his master took Anselm on, he would speak out. He was determined to ask if he might be allowed to retire.

"Now tell me about Sido de Villeduval."

Mr. Tull, hands behind his back, feet squarely apart, started. "The Laxtons live in Queen Square, in Bloomsbury. The house is well staffed and is a meeting place for many of the émigrés newly—"

"That interests me little. Tell me of the Marquise Sido."

"She is well cared for by her aunt and uncle. They are keen that she should master English and to that end she has lessons with a Mr. Trippen, an actor. She is taken to his house in Maiden Lane by sedan chair twice a week and is always accompanied by two servants. This same Mr. Trippen taught Yann Margoza." Mr. Tull, somewhat relieved that his other little enterprise appeared to be undiscovered and feeling braver, said, "I wonder if after this business I might be able to retire. It's just that . . ."

He didn't finish what he had to say, for Kalliovski's look of pure rage was enough to silence him.

"Once you work for me there is no retirement other than your own demise. You will await further instructions. When the time is right you will bring Sido de Villeduval here. Until then you are dismissed."

Back in the shop, Mr. Tull, feeling the weight of hell upon his shoulders, said to Milkeye, "Balthazar seems even bigger than when I last saw him."

Milkeye turned his one good eye on Tull. "Our master knows what you do. He knows that you and the butcher and his boy had a very profitable sideline. Don't think he doesn't."

"I don't know what you're talking about," said Mr. Tull, an icy sweat breaking out on his forehead.

Milkeye laughed. "You're walking on the edge, my friend. One false move and you will be Balthazar's next feast."

Mr. Tull had the decidedly uncomfortable feeling that his bones might already have been reserved for the design of a chandelier or mirror.

Milkeye followed him out to the street, where Mr. Tull breathed in the night air.

"Do you know why he still wants Sido de Villeduval?" he asked.

"If I were you, I wouldn't want to know. But I'll tell you this much: She's not all my master is after." A slow smile spread over his face. The effect was even more gruesome than usual. "The Marquise de Villeduval is only one part of his plan."

"What do you mean?" said Mr. Tull, feeling a shudder run down his spine.

Milkeye leaned forward, towering over him. "This is much harder to come by—some say impossible, but such an indifferent word has never stopped the count. He wants a key to a soul."

Mr. Tull looked down the rue des Couteaux with a longing to be gone from this madness and never return.

He thrust his shaking hands deep into his pockets. As he walked away he stumbled on a soft, unlikely thought. Under his breath he said, "Heaven help her. Heaven help all of us."

Chapter Eleven

The leather box containing the key sat waiting on Remon Quint's workbench. Even looking at it made his stomach churn. He regretted his lack of courage. He should have spoken out when he had the chance, told the man with the waxwork face and the poppy red gloves that what he desired was impossible, that no man on earth had the power to make a key to a soul. Speak the truth and shame the devil! But he hadn't. Instead he had listened, believing at first this was merely a rich man's foible. After all, he'd worked with enough clients whose wealth was beyond the realms of most men's understanding.

Usually flattery persuaded them to see that what they had purchased was unique. Yet he had the feeling that this man was in deadly earnest. Flattery would never satisfy his desire. He wanted a key to a soul and nothing else would do.

The key maker looked around his shabby apartment: a bedchamber, a workroom, and a small anteroom. These poky, lopsided chambers were all he could afford now. It was stiflingly hot; the smell of rubbish and rotten meat wafted through his open window. Today there was no breeze, just an unbearable, claustrophobic, sticky heat that made everyone irritable. Below he could hear the cobbler and his wife bickering.

He went to the cupboard and took out a half-empty bottle and a stale loaf, poured himself a glass of wine, carefully replaced the cork, broke off a piece of bread, and said grace, as he always did. For all his newfound poverty, he remained a pious man. He took a sip of the wine and grimaced. It was sour.

Before the Revolution, when the power of prayer was believed in, Remon Quint's prayers had been answered. He had owned a shop in the fashionable rue du Labon district, had a fine carriage and servants, wore elegant clothes and wigs, and was known for his hospitality. He could boast that he had dined with the king of key makers, Louis XVI, whose obsession was labyrinthine locks. Oh, how he had picked his brains to know their secret. Those were golden days.

He had entertained, held supper parties. When, with the dessert, he would bring out a mahogany toy guillotine, fashionable at the time, his guests delighted in taking turns to put little dolls under the knife and watch the miniature executions. The streams of red fluid that burst from them were merely perfume, to be caught on the handkerchiefs of giggling ladies.

How foolish to think nothing would change. Now everything was lost. They were ankle deep in blood.

The row between the cobbler and his wife had spilled into the courtyard. A man yelled at them from an upstairs window to shut up, otherwise they'd be for it.

Only a fool wouldn't know what was meant by that remark, thought the key maker. In this dog-eat-dog world, everyone was food for the tribunal, the tumbrel, and the guillotine. No man's neck was safe.

The key maker knew he was doomed. Maybe it would be best if he were arrested and taken to prison. His life was hanging by a thread, like a child's tooth.

One yank and it would be gone. At least in prison, he thought, there would be old friends to reminisce with, and he would be free at last to say what was on his mind.

It would make no difference. The guillotine would be waiting to embrace him whether he kept quiet or not. Instead here he was, at liberty, but lonely and wretched, plagued by voices in his head. This was Death's waiting room. Every time he heard a tread on the steps up to his apartment, he told himself it was the Grim Reaper.

If only he'd had the wit to leave after the fall of the Bastille as so many of his clients had done, conveniently forgetting to pay their bills. But he hadn't had the foresight to see what a revolution was capable of doing. He had agreed with those who were in favor of a constitutional monarchy. Once that was in place, the key maker was sure it would be business as usual. In a time of such political upheaval, instead of keeping an eye on events, he had buried himself in his work and refused to read the signs. He couldn't bring himself to believe that Paris could fall so low.

The toy guillotine had turned out to be no laughing matter. Its life-size version had sliced the heads off his most valuable customers, the convention confiscating their property so there was no possibility of claiming the monies he was owed.

He had been forced to close his shop. There hadn't been enough business to keep his fine house, his carriages or servants. He'd been told that his name was on a list of those suspected of having supplied the Duc d'Arlincourt with a lock for an iron chest in which pamphlets opposing the Republic had been discovered. Since he had been informed of this, he believed every day to be his last.

Three weeks ago, in the middle of the night, he had woken to find an apparition in his apartment, an immaculately dressed man sitting in his chair, his eyes closed. The key maker couldn't imagine what he was doing there, or whether or not he was dreaming, for the figure didn't look quite of this world. The raw scream hurt his throat as it made its embarrassed entrance into the room. The man in the chair opened his eyes. Dark and deadly, they were staring right through him.

"Citizen Quint," said this stranger, getting up and holding out a red-kid-gloved hand. "I have a commission for you."

He'd been given a month to create the impossible. He'd worked night and day, obliged to use a friend's furnace for the purpose. His whole life's work had gone into that one key. It was his masterpiece and in itself it held great beauty.

He had kept the design simple. Cast in silver, as requested, the bow was a circle in which stood a man, held in the wheel of life. The column was elegant and the bit was cut in the shape of the ace of spades. In this, if in nothing else, he had the measure of the man who commissioned it. But a key to a soul? What could he say? That such a thing was beyond him?

In a week's time the nocturnal visitor would return personally to collect it. The very thought of seeing him again had robbed the key maker of his reason, made him dizzy, as if the walls of the apartment were closing in on him. If they got any closer he would be squashed like an insect.

Then the voice had started, a woman's voice, gentle but insistent.

"The devil's own is on your trail. Run like the wind."

The words never changed. She never stopped, night and day, until the hinges of his reason loosened.

He staggered, clutching the sides of his head.

"Stop it," he shouted. "Stop it. I am not mad!"

Wide-eyed he looked at the door. Yes, that's what he needed, fresh air. He walked, then ran down the stairs. He had to get away. On the landing he bumped into the cobbler.

"Look where you're going," said the cobbler, then seeing the state of him, asked, "You all right, citizen? You're not going out like that, are you? You haven't got your shoes on."

Remon Quint saw nothing but the foot of the staircase. The voice in his head drowned the cobbler's words so that he appeared like a fish mouthing silently at him. Everything had slowed down. In the street he gasped for air, not knowing where he was or where he should be, and with the voice near shouting in his head it came to him what he must do. He had to drown out the sound.

He walked like a man possessed; even the cuts in his stockinged feet didn't register. At the Pont Neuf he stood looking down into the brown stained water of the Seine, like a man about to savor the first sip of a longed for cup of coffee.

Basco had been on an errand for Citizen Aulard. The tumbrels trundled past him, filled with the living dead, a drumbeat following them to their mass grave, a footnote to be forgotten in the folds of history. He took his time walking back to the Circus of Follies, thinking how much Paris had changed since the heady days of the fall of the Bastille, when everything had seemed brand-new, a clean page. Who would have imagined that the rest of the Revolution would be written in blood?

Citizens scurried past, heads down, terrified lest they be stopped, each believing the other to be a spy or an informer. Never had Basco known the city so starved of *joie de vivre*.

He was halfway across the Pont Neuf when he noticed a man without hat or shoes, and thought he was behaving strangely. But didn't everyone behave strangely these days?

Then he realized what Remon Quint was doing. As the key maker climbed onto the parapet of the bridge, Basco charged like a bull, desperate to get to him before it was too late. He saw him jump, heard a woman scream, saw an orange spill from her basket and roll away between the legs of passersby. He grabbed at what he prayed wasn't thin air and found he had the key maker dangling by his shirt.

"Let me go, please let me go. If you have any mercy, let me go."

Basco had no intention of doing so. Another man came to his aid and together they pulled the key maker back onto the bridge.

"I want to die," he said.

The crowd was already parting to let three National Guardsmen through.

"Papers," said one of the Bluecoats to Basco. "Now."

Basco, whose sense of his failure as an actor had been acute, thought little about outwitting the guard.

"My friend is very sick," he said. "He has a fever in the brain."

"Papers," repeated the guard, unimpressed.

Basco propped his new friend against the bridge as he struggled to find his documents.

The Bluecoat looked bored. Basco knew that bored officialdom was far more dangerous than occupied officialdom and these three were pushing for an arrest.

Then a woman screamed.

"Stop that man! He's stolen my bread! Stop, he's a ratbag of a Royalist!"

The guards, having found something worthy of their

attention, left Basco and rushed after the thief, swords and guns rattling.

Basco wasted no time. Heaving the key maker up like a sack of potatoes, and not a very heavy sack at that, he headed back to the safety of the Circus of Follies.

Chapter Twelve

"Bread and theaters, whatever next?" cried Citizen Aulard, his operatic eyebrows rising ever upward as his face fell like a curtain. "I am now expected to give free performances to distract the citizens of Paris from their rumbling stomachs. *Mort bleu!* In return for what? Worthless paper money!"

He stuffed his hands into his waistcoat pockets. Têtu, sitting with Iago, as usual, perched on top of his head, said nothing.

"What a wretched morning. A member of the Committee of Public Safety paid us a visit, inspected the theater, and wrote copious notes. Did you know that *eau de nil* green is an aristocratic color?"

He stared for a moment at the ceiling as if from it might come salvation.

"I've been ordered to repaint the auditorium. Please," he said tilting his head right back, "tell me when this stupidity will end. So many people dead, the prisons fit to bursting, and the scum of the streets now rule the country and want everything painted *bleu, blanc, rouge. Mort bleu!*"

"*Vive la Nation!*"

"Will you keep that parrot quiet? And that is another thing. *My* parrot, Iago. *My* parrot now seems to be your parrot and, what's more, is talking far too much."

He let out a heartfelt sigh and carried on with his list of woes, which were many.

"Why do they have to fiddle with everything? Three days of every decade, in this new calendar. Do you understand it?"

Citizen Aulard continued, not waiting for an answer, "No, it would be much better if they had kept the weeks, and just said that three days out of every ten we have to put on shows that will appeal to the empty stomachs of sans-culottes, to serve up a visual feast full of hot air and patriotic dribble. The other seven days we can do *The Harlequinade.*"

"This is very obliging of them," said Têtu.

"How so?"

"Because it gives us three days when Yann and Didier won't be missed. They'll stand a better chance of getting to the coast and back again before the next show."

"How long will all this go on for?" asked Citizen Aulard.

In truth the visit of the member of the Committee of Public Safety had made him realize just how vulnerable their operation was.

Quite what Têtu's answer would have been remained a mystery, for at that moment Basco and Yann entered the room. Between them they carried the semiconscious body of a shoeless middle-aged man.

Yann laid him on the day bed.

"I found him," said Basco, by way of explanation, "about to throw his life into the Seine."

"Oh wonderful, just what we need! And of course you thought straight away, I know, Citizen Aulard has hardly anything to do, and nothing to hide; I will take him to the Circus of Follies!"

"No, no, Signor Aulard, it wasn't like that," said Basco. "He was in trouble, no papers, and I thought—"

Citizen Aulard brought his fist down on the desk. "Heaven protect me from a thinking fencing master! What are we now? Home to every stray, barefoot citizen found perched on the Pont Neuf, about to answer to his maker?"

"That was not in my thinking," said Basco. "Yann said I should bring him here. I'd only intended to give him some brandy and some of my mother's homespun wisdom, then take him back to wherever he lives."

"And Yann, why did you bring him up here?"

"Because he has something on his mind that struck me as unusual."

"Have we all gone mad?"

"That's hard to know," said Yann. "Still, you don't often come across a shoeless man raving about how to make a key to a soul."

"What?" said Citizen Aulard.

"Quiet," said Têtu, "he's coming round."

Remon Quint sat up, looking the color of the auditorium. He was completely at a loss as to how he came to be surrounded by a strange assortment of people, one of whom was a dwarf with a parrot on his head.

"Do you remember your name?" asked Têtu.

"Yes. Remon Quint."

Citizen Aulard peered more closely at the man propping himself up on his day bed.

"No! Surely not the celebrated key maker from the rue du Lapon?" He adjusted his spectacles. "It cannot be. He is a very respected gentleman who wore, if my memory serves me well, the most handsome wigs and—"

"You know this man?" interrupted Têtu with surprise.

"Well, I know of him. He is a supreme craftsman. Of course, I never could afford one of his keys or locks. His customers were kings and princes. It was said that Marie Antoinette and King George of England commissioned keys from him."

"Thank you kindly, sir," said the key maker, "but all that was in another age, alas, all gone, washed away by the Revolution." He tried to stand. "Forgive me, I have inconvenienced you long enough and . . ." He stopped and stared in amazement at his stockinged feet as if they belonged to someone else. "Where are my shoes?"

"You didn't have them on at the Pont Neuf," said Basco.

"The Pont Neuf? What was I doing there?" He held the sides of his head.

"Shall I take you home?" asked Basco.

Remon Quint had round eyes in a large round head on a small neat body. He looked not unlike a stick balancing a ball. The memory of what he had been doing began to come back, and his eyes looked as if they were about to pop out of his head.

"I can't go back," he said. "The voice will return. This is the first time since *he* came that she's been silent."

"Would you like to tell us what the voice said?" asked Têtu, handing him a cognac, and knowing what the answer would be.

"She never stopped. She said, over and over again, 'The devil's own is on your trail. Run like the wind.'"

Yann broke the silence that greeted his words. "Anis," he said.

"It is an incredible story," said Citizen Quint. "Things like this don't happen, not to me. I am an ordinary man."

Citizen Aulard said, "We are all of a theatrical disposition here, and when I tell you that nothing is beyond the realms of possibility, I say it to comfort you and give you the courage to speak."

"You will think me mad. Perhaps I am."

"I think you are exhausted," said Têtu with such authority that the key maker felt his mind settling itself on the solid ground of rational thought.

So he started his story and he told it well; when he had finished you could have heard a pin drop.

"Where is the key now?" Yann asked Remon Quint.

"On my workbench." He stopped, took out his handkerchief, and mopped his forehead. "It's my finest work."

Yann set off across the Pont Neuf toward the rue de Rivoli. Here at the Pavillion de Marson was the noisome quarter of dingy houses intersected by narrow alleys, which extended from the rue St. Honoré to the Place du Carrousel. He found the house just as the key maker had described. It was a tall tenement building that looked as if it had been stretched upward to accommodate all its inhabitants; it hummed with life like a beehive.

Yann took his time and decided that it would be better observed from the café across the road, though when he entered the place, the smell of unwashed flesh and smoke made him instantly regret his decision. Having taken a table he felt that to leave straight away would draw unwanted attention to himself. Instead he peered through the steamed-up window.

Sobriety was a foreign word to the collection of drunks and misfits in the café, all of whom had the look of those who have sacrificed their souls to the bottle. The floor was covered in a matting of filthy sawdust, solid in parts where no one had the strength, or the will, to sweep it away.

To the disgust of the waiter, Yann ordered coffee. At the next table sat a man with a bright-red face. He was dressed in a worn cotton jacket, which had seen better days, and had a red cap on his head. He was in the middle of lecturing a citizeness who was only slightly less drunk than he. She at least wasn't slurring her words.

Yann watched the comings and goings of the building opposite, half listening to their conversation.

"No, woman, the way to feed the people is simple. We should be able to serve up aristocratic meat."

"What?" said the citizeness, sniffing. "How aristocratic? I don't mind where the blooming cow comes from as long as I have something to eat."

Yann wondered, if purgatory did exist, whether it would be a café like this.

"I tell you, woman, if the butcher Citizen Loup was still alive he would have done it, he would have sold meat from the guillotine." The man stopped to yell at the waiter for more brandy.

"That's disgusting," said the citizeness, spitting out her drink. "That makes me sick to my guts!"

"Well, woman, this city is plagued by famine. It's one way those stuffed-up, good-for-nothing, greedy, inbred aristos can bring about equality. After all, they eat only the very best food, so they should taste good."

"You are talking codswallop, you are."

"All right then, would you prefer that we kill all the cats and dogs to eat instead?"

"That would be a daft thing to do."

"Why? Cat and dog not to your taste?"

"No, all I mean is, if we did that, what would kill the rats?"

The sans-culotte, realizing that he'd been gotten the better of, grunted. "The trouble with you, woman, is that your brains don't work." He turned to Yann for support. "But it doesn't matter, does it, because we're all going to be equal."

"Equal in what?" asked Yann. "For you say that you

have a better brain than your companion, so if you're right, where is the equality?"

"Take no notice, citizen," said the woman. "It's just a bee in his bonnet. Equality? I can't see it myself."

Yann asked, "Have you heard the one about the king who made all men equal by the simple means of an iron table?"

"No. How?"

"Everyone who came to his kingdom was forced to lie on the iron table. If you were too short for it, your legs would be stretched on the rack; if you were too long for it, your legs would be chopped off to fit. That way the king could guarantee all men were equal."

The man looked foxed. "I don't understand."

"Neither did anyone who had to lie on the iron table, but they all had to live with the crippling consequence."

The woman burst out laughing. "Are you a comedian?" she asked.

Yann drank up his coffee and paid his bill. "No, I leave that to the likes of your friend here, with his taste in meat."

The citizen lurched to his feet. "You're making fun of me. No one makes fun of me. I will show you equality, and you too, woman, if you don't shut your trap." He went to take a swing at Yann. Mysteriously, he missed his footing and fell flat on his face.

The waiter rushed forward as Yann, stepping over the prostrate man, winked at the woman, who sat there chuckling.

Outside, the sun hit the narrow street in intense strips of light. A line for bread stretched all the way around the corner. A scuffle had started by the door of the baker's shop between two women fighting tooth and claw over a loaf of bread. The crowd, bored with waiting, goaded them on.

We have become a city of scavengers, thought Yann as he slipped into a small, dark courtyard, an open mouth stinking of bad breath. A door led to wooden stairs that twisted and turned unevenly. His footsteps were the beat of a drum. The smell of animal fat, rotten vegetables, tobacco, and tallow candles hung thick and sickly in the air. He heard a noise on the ground floor, a door opening and closing, an argument, a man's voice shouting. Above him, a quieter *click*—the kind of noise you make when you don't want to be heard. Someone was coming out of the key maker's apartment. Yann pressed himself against the wall and caught a glimpse of a face he recognized glancing over the banister. If the owner of the milky eye had any vision in it, he might have seen him, despite the gloom of the stairwell. He heard Milkeye start to walk down he stairs.

Yann, knowing there was nowhere to conceal himself, acted quickly. Têtu always said the best place to hide is under the noses of those who want to find you.

He slumped to the floor, almost blocking the stairs, pulled his hat over his face and started muttering drunken patriotic drivel. Milkeye took no notice of him, except to kick his legs aside so that he could pass, at which the drunk let out an expletive for having been so rudely disturbed. The sound of his voice spurred Milkeye to move with greater speed down the creaking steps, taking them two at a time. Yann heard the door close behind him. He waited to make sure Milkeye wasn't coming back before going into the key maker's apartment.

The place had been ransacked. The key was gone.

Yann stood among the wreckage feeling as if he had been punched in the chest. What a fool he had been. How many signs did he need before he acknowledged his worst fear?

Now seeing Milkeye again he had no doubt: Kalliovski

must still be alive. Not for the first time he wondered if luck was on his side. Perhaps Têtu was right. He needed the talisman. Ever since he'd heard the dog howling at the Duc de Bourcy's château, he'd known the spirit of Anis was trying to warn him. Again, fate was gambling with his life.

He looked up at the tobacco-stained ceiling. "Kalliovski," he said out loud, "let this be between you and me, no one else. Leave Sido be."

He left the apartment—there was nothing to be done there—and looked down the stairwell to make sure the coast was clear. At the bottom, a door opened.

"Who are you?" said a man, reaching out to stop Yann.

"What is it to you, citizen?"

"Everything. I know everything that goes on in this building."

"Well, you don't, citizen, otherwise you would know that Remon Quint's apartment has been burgled."

"What's happening, Brutus?" came a female voice from inside.

"Burgled, then? Maybe I just caught the villain who did it," said the man, grabbing hold of Yann's coat.

Often Yann saw people's minds as market stalls: all

the thoughts in their heads put out on display. This shoemaker's mind, pickled in wine, was so simple that he knew exactly what he was thinking.

"You should take your hands off me, citizen," said Yann, "unless you want me to report you. I know you're still making shoes for the counterrevolutionaries."

Rats scurry away into dark places when they hear footsteps, and so did the shoemaker. At the word *counterrevolutionaries*, he disappeared.

Chapter Thirteen

The banker Charles Cordell arrived at the theater around midnight. He was a tall, bespectacled man, with a broken buttress of a nose and gray eyes that looked as if they had stared at too many facts and figures, and found that nothing in life added up.

In the early days of the Revolution he'd been one of its most ardent supporters, but long before the execution of Louis XVI, he realized it had become a monstrous excuse for cruelty. The clever talk, the velvet-tongued justification of such acts in the name of liberty, equality, and fraternity, mattered little. The truth, as far as he was concerned, was far less palatable and altogether more basely human: vengeance, jealousy, and greed.

Unlike many of his fellow Englishmen, he had stayed in Paris when war with England had been declared. With a rabbit foot for good luck in his coat pocket, he hadn't been arrested yet. But he had a feeling that time was not on his side.

He and Citizen Aulard were engrossed in conversation when Yann entered the room. Cordell paused, wondering if the candlelight was playing tricks. For a moment he could have sworn that Yann had a myriad of brightly colored threads dancing all around him.

He closed his eyes and when he looked again they had gone. There was only the room, the candlelight, and Yann. But then again, he thought, many strange things happen around this young man. It was as if he weaved between two worlds: this one, blood-soaked and ruined, and another altogether more mysterious.

"Do you know the Silver Blade's reputation is growing in London? You are quite a hero in émigré society," said Cordell.

"That sounds worrying," said Têtu, close behind Yann. He was more than aware of the speculation, not only in London but in Paris, as to the identity of the Silver Blade.

"The good thing is that no one can quite remember

who you are, or for that matter what you look like. Would it be presumptuous to ask how you do that?"

"Too much is made of it," answered Yann. "Where is Remon Quint?"

"Basco is sitting with him," said Citizen Aulard. "Citizen Quint is quiet. Sleep is the best remedy."

"Did he say anything else about the key?" asked Yann.

"He genuinely believes that he is going to be killed the minute he hands over his masterpiece."

"Why?" asked Cordell.

"Because he was commissioned to make a key to a soul."

"And what on earth does that mean?" asked Citizen Aulard. "Yes, you can have a key to a door, a key to a city, the keys of a kingdom, but never a key to the soul. Such a thing is impossible." He puffed his cheeks, letting a *put-put* noise out through his mouth, and exclaimed, "*Mort bleu!* You are a rational man, Mr. Cordell, you don't believe all this nonsense?"

There was silence, then Cordell asked, "Where is this key?"

"He left it in his apartment," said Yann, "but it is no longer there. I saw Milkeye leaving—he'd ransacked the place. The key was commissioned by Count Kalliovski."

The theater manager sat down heavily in his seat. "No, no! He was killed in the September Massacre. Please tell me he was killed." An awful idea dawned on him. "Do you think Kalliovski and the so-called phantom who walks in the Place de la Révolution are one and the same?"

Yann didn't reply, for Cordell's thoughts worried him.

"What report?" Yann asked.

Cordell sighed. "Nothing much escapes you, does it?"

"Forgive me, that was rude," said Yann, "but this report, whatever it is, is much on your mind."

"Correct. I had a spy working for me and Laxton, here in Paris, whose brief was to infiltrate a secret society believed to be operating under the city. His dispatches made intriguing reading indeed. The spy, a man by the name of Levis Artois, reported that the meetings took place in the catacombs, in a large domed cavernous room made entirely of human bones. A man known simply as the master is the head of this organization, a terrifying figure of demonic power."

Cordell looked grave. "The last message I received from Artois was to say that he was sending me a report with further information about the master, and the names of several of his followers. Many, he indicated, worked in positions of high office, in the Convention and the Committee of Public Safety. Unfortunately, the report never reached me."

"What happened?" asked Citizen Aulard.

"A body was fished out of the Seine about a week ago. There was little left to identify it. It had been torn to pieces by a monstrous beast. But I suspect it was Artois."

Têtu had been silent. Of all of them, he understood the dreadful significance of Cordell's story.

"Remon Quint should be escorted from Paris to London," he said. "I don't think it would be wise to leave him at Dieppe. If he is as important to Kalliovski as we believe, the count will have his men waiting at the ports to find him. Yann should go with him all the way to London."

"I suppose he could do that successfully while the theater is being repainted," said Citizen Aulard.

But Yann wasn't listening. His mind was whirling. London. He would be able to see Sido. Sido—at last.

He did his best to keep the excitement out of his voice. "That will work."

"Before we agree," said Cordell, "I have something to say and it must be said now. The situation in Paris is going to get worse. I have heard rumors that a proposal to accelerate the Terror is to be put forward to the convention this month."

"That is ridiculous—" Citizen Aulard began.

"Please," interrupted Cordell. "I want to know if you all wish to continue with assignments, or would you rather we disband now?"

"No," said Yann firmly. "We should go on. To stop now would be the coward's way."

"Yannick," said Têtu, "consider Cordell's proposal. You have helped more than enough people escape. Now is the time to return to England, to take up your place at Cambridge."

Yann looked at Têtu, bewildered. "Are you all right?"

"Yes, quite well. What do you think, Citizen Aulard?"

"Have I missed something? Because I don't understand your reasoning," said the theater manager, perplexed.

"This business has always been dangerous. If we were to close down now and vanish in the night, we would be

167

deserting many who need us. And why is Yann at more risk than before?"

"I was just testing your commitment, that's all."

No, you weren't, thought Yann. You have seen the future.

It was about one thirty when the small meeting dispersed. Yann waited until he was alone with Têtu.

"Is Death walking with me?" he asked

"I wish you knew more of the Gypsy ways. I wish I had taught you better."

"Têtu, answer me."

"But did I tell you that bridges are important? They straddle two worlds, and you walk with ease between them, but do you spit into the water before you cross? All Gypsies know they must do that. There is a saying: 'I believe that by the bridge of Cin-Vat all good deeds will be rewarded and evil deeds punished.' Whatever Kalliovski has done belongs to evil. It is a bridge too unstable to cross more than once. And I am frightened for you, Yannick, very frightened indeed."

Tears welled in his eyes and Yann felt cold inside. He'd never seen Têtu like this.

"It will be all right," he said reassuringly. "Next time, I will remember to spit."

He rested his hand on Têtu's shoulder.

With a heavy heart Yann made his way to his attic home and climbed out onto the roof. He would often sit and look out over the sleeping city, at its ramshackle rooftops, its lopsided chimneypots, and church spires pointing into the night sky.

Shirkis. The Romany word for stars—birds of fire that only fly in darkness. He remembered how Têtu used to sing to him when he was small.

And the moon, the lady of the heavens coming nightly,
certain in her coming o'er the meadow just to feed her chickens.

And Yann thought, I am like a bird of fire. Free at last, coming to tell you I love you, Sido. I love you.

Chapter Fourteen

It was another hot evening when the curtain rose on the last performance of *The Harlequinade* before the theater was to close for repainting.

Remon Quint was better than he had been, but worry had eaten at him, and his eyes had a hunted look. Even Didier, who had no ability to read minds, could see that this man was close to the breaking point. They sat together under the stage waiting for Yann, the key maker locking and unlocking his fingers.

When the curtain fell, the audience was in no mood to let Harlequin go. Flowers were thrown on the stage; from the balcony a woman declared her undying love for him. The curtain was lifted again and again, until finally it rested for the last time, its velvet folds still quivering as Yann made a sprint for the door. Removing his mask, he rushed to join Didier and the key maker below stage.

From the minute they descended the stone stairs leading to the catacombs, Yann was filled with foreboding. The key maker was shaking.

"I'm not good in small spaces . . . I . . ."

"You have to trust us," said Yann, but he was aware of a bad feeling fogging his mind. As much as he tried to force it away, he knew it was not a good omen, and omens were important to his Gypsy soul. The key maker looked almost wild with fright by the time they entered the catacombs.

"I can't do it," he announced. "I can't stand the idea of all that earth above me. All the weight of the buildings pressing down, all the bones of the dead . . . all the worms . . . I have to go back. I have to. I'm going to be buried alive down here. I know it."

Yann gently held his arm and, his voice a lullaby, said quietly, "Look at me."

The key maker stared at him, and in those ebony eyes he found, as little Louis had before him, a stillness like calm water.

"Do you think he'll be all right?" asked Didier.

"I hope so."

They set off, Yann in front, Didier at the rear, their lights swaying back and forth, gently illuminating the distance that lay ahead. Their plan was to reach the Chamber of Sighs, then stop for a rest. Yann had named the vaulted cavern after the words painted neatly on the wall: *Life is a circle of sighs.* It was the first landmark he'd found in his search for a route out of the city.

They walked, keeping their heads down. It was wet underfoot. The catacombs were given to weeping and this evening the tunnels wept. All that could be heard in this echo-less place was the splash of their shoes.

But Yann couldn't shake off the feeling that something was wrong. He began to sense that they were being followed. He turned several times to confront the darkness, convinced he heard the panting of a great beast. He shone his light back the way they had come. He could see nothing, just the same empty tunnels. Didier too looked back.

"What is it?"

"Nothing," said Yann, but he sensed something evil closing in.

At the Chamber of Sighs, they rested and took water and food from their knapsacks. They always carried enough oil to keep the lamps lit for eight hours, for without light they would never find their way out again. Yann had long ago explored the Chamber of Sighs, a dead end that led nowhere, but it was a good place to stretch after walking hunched up for so long. There was a stone bench and here they sat in silence.

The key maker was eating and drinking like a sleepwalker, when suddenly he let out a terrified scream, sending a chill through Yann's soul.

On the wall opposite loomed the shadow of an enormous dog.

Remon Quint was in a frenzy. He darted into the darkness of the vaulted room with Didier and Yann in pursuit.

"He can't get far," Yann was saying, but to their amazement the key maker disappeared. Yann was surprised to see a gap in what he had always thought was a solid wall. They found themselves in a large unmapped tunnel ablaze with the light of candles gripped in bony fingers, coated in dripping wax. There was neither hide nor hair of the key maker.

"Where the hell are we?" asked Didier. "What do we do?"

The sound of the dog's barking was loud and close.

"We should split up. You go that way, I'll go this, and I'll meet you back here. We have to find him."

Yann drew his knife and made a cross on the wall. As he set off down the long hall, a rush of wind blew out the candles, even extinguishing his oil lamp.

Powerless in the dark, he was trying to relight his lantern when he heard a rustle of silk.

"Calico and corpses."

An icy hand touched his.

"Sisters Macabre, is it you?" he asked the endless darkness.

Something snowflake-soft stroked his face. Holding his nerve, he tried once more to relight his lantern. Every time, the flame would flicker and die.

"Damask and death."

"Where are you?" he asked.

"Where we should be."

"Where you belong."

Finally the flame took, and light spilled out, and to his great relief he could see.

"Tulle and truth."

Before him stood the Seven Sisters Macabre, lined up against the wall of the chamber, as hideous to behold as they always had been, their faces powdered, their cheeks rouged, their skin patched, their lips sewn closed. At their throats the infamous red necklaces. Their voices came from inner ghosts. They moved toward him, their feet not touching the ground. They glided. Yet Yann could see no threads of light. How were they being worked?

"We knew we would see you again.

"For you belong to us."

Yann didn't move. Slowly they glided closer. He tried with all his willpower to take control of them, but he could not.

"We are not yours anymore," said one.

Their flesh smelled of dead lilies.

"What do you want?" asked Yann. They began to whirl around him, their faces a blur, their skulls showing through their stitched, papery skin.

They spoke with one eerie voice: "Your father is waiting. He has been waiting a long, long time."

In that moment, that last moment when Yann's future still shone so full of promise, before fate turned his dreams to ashes, in those last seconds when loving Sido was still possible, Yann wished he had the power to stop the clocks.

His words tasted of clay. "My father? He is dead."

"Count Kalliovski is waiting to embrace you. You, his one and only son."

No sooner were the words spoken than somewhere close by, the monstrous dog howled.

"Your father doesn't like to be kept waiting," whispered the Sisters Macabre.

Chapter Fifteen

Count Kalliovski's new toy, the head of the Marquis
de Villeduval, sat on a small ebony table in its glass
case. Kalliovski's passion, if not obsession, was the
making of automata. He was striving to create a being
without the inconvenience of a soul, and with each
one of his creations he believed himself to be nearing
his ambition.

The marquis was manipulated, like the count's many
other automata, by the dark threads. Today, the head
gazed at the long gallery, with its tall windows and
the painted scenery of the gardens where the air was
filled with birdsong, so like the vistas he had looked
on in life. The count sat in a wing-back chair, his legs
stretched, his red kid gloves like a blazing spire before

his mouth. Balthazar lay beside him, his huge head resting on his paws.

"Shall I tell you my plans, my mad friend?" said Kalliovski.

"Have you woken me to bore me with information that holds little fascination for me?"

"No, you cake stand of a head. I am here to tell you what designs I have on your daughter, remember her?"

"I have no daughter," said the Marquis de Villeduval. "I never had any children. I don't like them."

"Then I will tell you what I intend for your niece, Sido de Villeduval."

"I have no niece. I once knew a Sidonie, an exceptionally plain girl with a limp. Speak to yourself about her if you must. I am engaged in an altogether more amusing subject."

Controlling his creation's speech afforded Kalliovski much pleasure. He sat back feeling all-powerful, delighted with this head of his. A thin smile crept across his face.

"I see nothing to merit such mirth," said the Marquis de Villeduval. "And, as I said, you are interrupting an interesting train of thought about snuffboxes."

"Not shoe buckles, my dear marquis?"

"What use is a shoe buckle to a severed head?"

Kalliovski's laughter rang throughout the long gallery.

"It matters little. I will tell you all the same. I have forged a deal with the devil, and Sido will ensure its success. She will be my pretty little caged dove. I shall use her to lure me a falcon. And when I have him, I shall steal his soul, and the threads of light will be mine. I've had a key made for that very purpose. What do you say to that, surveyor of snuffboxes?"

"My ears are stuffed with wax," said the Marquis de Villeduval. "I cannot hear you."

"My dear demented sir, there is no escape from me. I told you long ago, just as I told Sido. I have no mercy. I show no mercy. I never forget what is owing to me, what belongs to me."

The marquis's spirit, a moth imprisoned inside the head, was fluttering at broken memories.

"You are like me," he said. "We are both quite mad."

Kalliovski stared incredulously at his creation, who dared to speak of his own free will. In quiet rage he sent out the dark threads. Slowly, as if squeezing juice from an orange they robbed the marquis of all independent speech. Quiet now, his eyes snapped tight shut.

"Oh, my dear foolish marquis. What? Silent at last?" said Kalliovski, closing the door on the waxwork head.

He thought he saw one unorchestrated tear roll down the marquis's puffy cheeks.

He rang the bell and Milkeye entered.

"Where is the key maker?"

"Citizen Quint is in the workroom, master."

"Then tonight it will begin. Send Anselm Loup to me."

How many days or weeks Anselm had been in Kalliovski's wondrous domain he couldn't rightly say, nor did he much care, for as long as he was never asked to leave, he didn't mind.

Every day he had been called to the long gallery to sit before his new master. And every day he found himself coming out of a trance and feeling different, as if the furniture of his mind had been shifted. His feelings, whatever they had been, for his adoptive father, the butcher Loup, were now replaced by a passionate devotion to Count Kalliovski.

Soon after this transfer of affection, an idea came to Anselm, independent, or so it seemed, of all that his master had planted in the fertile plains of his uneducated mind. Perhaps he was Kalliovski's bastard son, for they had much in common, and hadn't he been abandoned at birth? As his master said, everything has a design, everyone a destiny.

The day Kalliovski put his long-awaited plan into action, Anselm arrived in his master's presence brimming with enthusiasm. He was much changed from the day when Mr. Tull had first taken him there. His hair was coiffed, his skin shiny clean, and his clothes tailored especially for him. He looked every inch a hero: blond hair, amber eyes, a slayer of dragons, a breaker of hearts.

The count studied him and said, "If you fail me in this assignment, it will be the last you are given as a living man."

Anselm felt his throat tighten. He wouldn't fail.

"There is a small theater company called the Circus of Follies. I want you to find out what goes on there," said Kalliovski.

Anselm looked bewildered. The question "How?" sat uncomfortable and unspoken on his lips.

"I suggest you capitalize on your assets—your looks. There is a girl, her name is Colombine, she is the leading actress. Through her you will find out all I need to know about the dwarf Têtu and, more importantly, Yann Margoza. Succeed in this and you will be my day, as I am the night."

That afternoon Anselm found himself once more in the rue des Couteaux, with only the vaguest of memories of where he had been, and an overwhelming desire to meet an actress called Colombine.

Chapter Sixteen

Têtu had been working late and knew something was wrong even before he saw Yann standing on the landing, his face white, his clothes covered in limestone chalk.

"What are you doing here? Where's Didier?" Têtu asked, darting a glance behind Yann. "Is he with you?"

"No."

"And Remon Quint?"

"I don't know."

"What do you mean, you don't know? Are they safe?"

"Why did you never tell me the truth? All this time . . . all those lies."

Têtu was frightened by the look on Yann's face. "What has happened, Yannick? Tell me now."

"No, first you owe me the truth. Is Kalliovski my father?"

"Who did you hear that from?" Têtu's voice was less assured.

"My friend," said Yann coldly, "time is running out. I'm a fool to have trusted you. How many times did I ask you who my father was? And all you did was lie."

"No, no, I didn't lie. He was a Gypsy. I just didn't name him."

"If I remember rightly, you told me my father was dead."

"And again I didn't lie."

"I suppose that depends on what you call the truth."

"Every truth is just one man's story, Yannick. You can believe whatever story you want."

"I don't want some fairy tale." Yann was shaking with rage. "I want the truth."

"Tell me what has happened to the key maker. I need to know," said Têtu, with a rising sense of panic.

"I don't care. Does that surprise you? I don't care. Lord knows how angry I am. I've a mind to kill you—you, whom I trusted completely. You, whom I believed to be my friend, you, whom I love. How could you do this to me? Why hadn't you the courage to say who my father was when I asked? It would have been better then, when there was nothing to lose—"

He stopped. A lump in his throat made speaking difficult. "How do I live with this? How can I ever be with Sido, knowing what I know? Now my life hangs by this thread. The devil take you—I want the truth."

Têtu moved toward him.

"Don't touch me! Leave me be."

"Listen, listen!" shouted Têtu, turning red in the face. "Kalliovski originally came from Transylvania to France. When I first met him in St. Petersburg, he was a poor young Gypsy with a pack of cards and a hatred for his own kind."

"You have told me before that Kalliovski was born a Gypsy, but I don't know if I believe a word of it. That could be another lie. After all, Kalliovski killed our people for sport. How can I trust a word you say?"

"I have proof," said Têtu.

"What proof?"

"I met his people. I knew his family."

"When were you ever in Transylvania?"

"Yann, stop this!"

"No, I want to know. When were you ever in Transylvania?"

"When I owned a dancing bear."

"A dancing bear? If I weren't so angry, I would be laughing."

"'There are many earths on earth there be.' You, a Gypsy, know this. You have evidence of it in the gifts you were given. Look at what you can do! How many men can work the threads of light? Some would say that none can. Is that the truth? Yes, in a way, because few have the ability to see such threads. Tell me, does that mean they don't exist?"

"And this," said Yann, feeling every nerve in his body on fire, "is supposed to comfort me? Well, it doesn't."

"Your mother believed the spirit of her Gypsy bridegroom was in you, even if Kalliovski is your father by blood. In her eyes, you were never his child. She told me you were the ghost-child of her one and only true love, a Gypsy called Manouche. If you wish to think of Kalliovski as your father, you will be giving him a power he has no right to—"

"I hate you for keeping the truth from me!" cried Yann. "I despise you for it. When were you planning to tell me? Sometime? Never?" He punched the wall.

"You must try to calm down," said Têtu. "Go to London as planned. Tell Sido what has happened."

Yann laughed, a dead, hollow sound. "No wonder, Têtu, that you thought we should disband and I go back to England. Did you think this might all disappear, that I would never find out?"

Têtu was silent.

"How did my mother die? I think you told me . . . that's right, my *father* murdered her."

"I understand how upset you are, but once you have thought about—"

"You could never in a lifetime understand how I feel."

Yann slumped into a chair, his head in his hands.

"I never told you because I was worried that it would destroy you. I have brought you up since you were an infant. I have never seen even a shadow of Kalliovski in you. The more you have grown, the more I believed Anis was right; you are indeed the child of her lost love Manouche. She made me swear never to tell you, so that Kalliovski wouldn't have any power over you."

Yann took a deep breath. "By my father's hand, I am cursed for life."

Têtu sighed. "Don't go down that path, Yannick. You have all before you." He went over to the desk. "This letter arrived today."

Yann took the envelope and looked at Sido's writing. He handed the letter back.

"It's over," he said. "These letters are not safe. There will be no more." He was shaking with rage. "Do you think I don't know that Juliette Laxton is terrified of her niece being in love with a Gypsy? Let alone the son of the monster who tried to abduct her."

"Yann, please, I know I counseled you against this liaison but love is precious and it has given you so much strength. Think of what this will do to Sido."

"By my father's hand, I am destroyed. What is left is nothing. Yes, it will break her heart. I now know how that feels—my heart is broken. But she will recover. Sooner or later, someone will tell her I am Kalliovski's son. The Laxtons will sigh with relief that their niece was saved from such an ill-advised liaison. One day she will meet a good man, marry, be happy, and tell her children how once a Gypsy boy saved her life in the days of the French Revolution."

"Yannick," said Têtu. "Go to London and see her."

"What could Sido possibly say? That it changes nothing?" Yann got up and went toward the door. Têtu saw he was trembling. "What is the point? There is nothing left."

"Where are you going?"

"Here is another truth for you, Têtu. There are a lot of men out there who are the walking dead. Tonight I join them."

"Don't let Kalliovski win," said Têtu. "He wants to destroy you as he destroyed your mother. Don't let this ruin your future. You're Manouche's ghost-child. Kalliovski was born with hatred and jealousy at the very root of him, like a rotten tree. You don't have to be his poisoned fruit."

Yann looked back at Têtu. He seemed suddenly even smaller, as if he had shrunk, and Yann felt himself to have grown too big for the room. He had become a giant in anger. He needed air.

"Where are you going?" asked Têtu again.

"To get drunk."

Têtu watched him leave, tears streaming down his face. "Anis, what should I do? Tell me, what should I do?"

Later that night Didier wearily made his way back into the theater. He found Têtu sitting at Citizen Aulard's desk, his face tear-stained, looking as old as Time itself.

"Is Yann back?" Didier asked.

"Yes."

Têtu poured them both a glass of cognac.

"Where's Remon Quint?"

"I don't know," said Didier, moving his shoulders back and rolling his head around his neck. He was stiff all over. He took the glass. "We lost him down there. I searched and searched, but I couldn't find him. It's not good, is it?"

"No."

"I could go down again."

"You will never find him. It's too late."

"It can't be."

"But it is," said Têtu, knowing the key maker was already beyond help. He could only hope that Yann had the strength for the battle ahead.

"I'm very sorry we failed Remon Quint," said Didier gravely.

"So am I," said Têtu.

"Where's Yann now?"

"Gone out."

"That's unlike him."

"Yes," replied the dwarf.

In the Café du Coin the company of actors was celebrating its last performance. Colombine had just met a young man who seemed to be devoted to her. Tonight Anselm was capitalizing on his newly discovered assets.

"Come on," shouted Basco, "give us another song."

And standing on a table Colombine sang, her voice not strong, but sweet with an innocence that she had never possessed.

Yann knew he had chosen the wrong place the minute he opened the door.

A stagehand rushed over. "Yann," he said, louder than he meant to. "What has happened? Why are you back?"

Looking around the smoky room, Yann noticed Colombine's latest conquest and instinctively sensed the darkness around him.

Anselm glanced in Yann's direction and recognized him immediately. This was the young man who'd killed his pa.

Yann walked past the stagehand to the bar. "I'm thirsty, that's all."

Colombine, who had been lifted off the table, rushed over to him. Anselm watched closely. Her obvious interest in Yann only made her more desirable.

Yann drank up, not wishing to stay longer than necessary. He wanted to find a bar where he would be guaranteed some peace.

"Don't leave. You've only just arrived," said Colombine, sensing that something was wrong.

Ignoring her, he handed the barman a roll of *assignats*, then turned to the rest of the company and said, "Well done, everybody. Have a drink on me." And with that he was gone.

Colombine picked up her shawl to follow him.

"Where are you going?" asked Anselm, grabbing hold of her arm.

"Let go of me."

"Not until you tell me where you're going."

"That's none of your business. Take your hands off me."

"What? A lovers' tiff already?" asked Pantalon.

Colombine shook her arm free, to see two white marks where Anselm's fingers had gripped her.

"Look what you've done!" she said, and slapped him hard.

Red, raw rage surged through Anselm. His fingers itched to break every bone in her body. The longing was almost beyond his control. Only a small voice inside his head willed him to be still.

Colombine flounced out of the café.

"Have another drink," said Basco, putting his arm around Anselm. "Take no notice, that one has broken more hearts than the guillotine has cut off heads."

Yann meanwhile walked toward the Seine, his hands stuffed in his pockets. He crossed the Pont Neuf and reached the Café des Amis. The owner knew Yann well and was pleased to see him.

"Not many out tonight," he said. "We've missed you. You don't come this way so often since you left the rue du Temple."

Yann nodded, took a bottle over to the table by the window, sat down, and poured himself a glass.

Damn Têtu. Damn all the lies, damn the Revolution. Damn everything. He poured himself another drink. How can I live with this? Tell me that, Yann Margoza, son of Count Kalliovski?

He downed his drink in one gulp. If I've inherited anything from my father, I'd better hope that it's his ability to feel nothing. Keep tipping this vinegary muck down and nothing is all I will ever feel. Nothing is all I will ever be.

Why him? I could cope with a coward, a traitor, a fool—but not Kalliovski.

Yann looked down at the bottom of his glass and refilled it.

What is it that Pantalon always says? "Life is a bottle of wine. The art is to make it last and to know how to enjoy it." I don't want it to last. The sooner the bottle is empty the better.

"Can I join you?"

He looked up to see Colombine.

"Why aren't you with the others?"

She slid down next to him. "I thought you looked sad. And something has gone wrong, I can tell."

He laughed. "What about golden boy? Won't he be a bit fed up that you've gone?"

"He's nothing to me."

"Does anybody mean anything to you?"

"Yes. You do," she said, looking wistfully at him.

Yann finished his drink.

Anselm had left shortly after Colombine and followed her, knowing she would lead him to Yann Margoza.

He couldn't care less about Colombine, except that he had been ordered to win her trust. That was easy. If he wanted her, she was his and he knew it. No, the challenge lay with Yann Margoza. He was everything

194

Anselm longed to be. What he would give to possess Yann's powers.

Through the window of the Café des Amis, he watched Colombine and Yann for a few minutes. Then, sweat gleaming on his face, he went in and sat down with them.

"I am Anselm, citizen," he said extending a hand to Yann.

Yann, paying no notice of the gesture, got up and walked unsteadily to the door. He turned toward them. "Good night."

Anselm tried to follow him, but Colombine pulled him back. If she couldn't have Yann, let him at least see what he was rejecting. She quickly kissed Anselm, whose eyes were fixed on Yann's retreating figure. He wanted to throw her off, to punish her for her cheek, but Kalliovski's words were an anchor in his stormy mind. *Make the girl yours and the rest will follow.* Anselm kissed her back violently.

Chapter Seventeen

The next morning, Yann woke on the forest floor, his head thudding. He looked at the sky. The sun shone bright through the canopy of transparent leaves, as if it were the emerald stained-glass window of a great cathedral. A choir of insects buzzed and the day was already warm. He felt in his pocket and found a coin. Having no idea which direction to take, he flipped it and let fate lead him.

His anger with himself, with everything, was the spur that kept him walking. He tried not to think of Sido, which proved impossible.

Leaves, he said to himself, watching one young leaf fall from an oak tree. Leaves for a while must think they own the skies, that they are close to heaven. When do they resign themselves to gravity? I am like a leaf. I believed I owned the sky without realizing that I'm destined to fall to the ground.

He noticed neither rain nor sun. His tangle of thoughts slowly unwound so that by the afternoon, he could feel enough to know he was hungry. He hunted rabbits and ate berries. At night, with a fire going and his food on a spit, he felt himself like the king of fools. The stars were the painted roof of this wondrous palace he had found. He paid no attention to his route. If he saw a hamlet or smoke from a farmhouse chimney, he made sure he took a large detour. If uncertain which way to go, he tossed a coin.

Days passed in this way until early one misty morning, emerging from a forest, he saw a gilded armchair left standing, its stuffing oozing out as if it had been mortally wounded, its dainty carved wooden legs bravely sunk into the carpet of leaves. Ivy had already wrapped around it, anchoring it to the earth.

Walking past it, he came to a gravel drive. Several of the trees on either side were burned, their skeleton limbs outstretched like ancient timber that had been turned to stone by what they had witnessed, for all that remained of the château was rubble.

He meandered around outbuildings, through the empty stables, down to the overgrown garden, to see flapping in the breeze a lady's dress, poised like a butterfly on a box hedge, its silver bows catching the first rays of warm sunlight. It fluttered, waiting for a gust of wind to free it, to take flight.

Why the chair and why the dress? Why, out of everything that must have been here, had they alone survived?

As he turned to leave, he spied a child's wooden horse lying on its side in a stream, one of its wheels turning occasionally.

He found these three objects profoundly moving: small mysterious relics of lives destroyed. He lifted the wooden horse out of the water. All the paint had washed away from the side that had been in the stream. He imagined this horse was once beloved by a child who had refused to leave it behind until it became a burden.

He freed the dress, light as gossamer, and it nearly fell to pieces in his hands. He took it and the wooden horse back to the armchair and left them there: an altarpiece to a vanquished world.

He carried on walking. By late afternoon he was grateful to come to a lake surrounded by cornfields. In the far distance a row of poplars cast long sleepy shadows. He sat contemplating the still waters before undressing and diving in, swimming lazily back and forth, as a moorhen, in ruffled indignation, took flight. Dragonflies skimmed the surface of the lily leaves, flashes of incandescent emerald and sapphire. He floated on his back, hypnotized by the sky, before emerging from the water and dressing.

He made his way through a cornfield dotted with dancing bright red poppies, rubies among the gold. The air was filled with birds, and it came to him then and there, a revelation of sorts. He said it out loud.

"The love I have for Sido is not diminished by what has happened, nor by who my parents were. It is stronger. Even if I can never see her again, never be with her, this much I know, a truth as bright and yellow as the corn, as red and passionate as the poppies: I have loved and been loved in return. I can find the strength to set her free. I can do this, for true love must have at its very soul the power to let go, and to know that nothing is lost."

Yann was crying. He realized he was not alone. A little way off he could see the figures of a man and woman. They were brightly dressed as if going to a fete, their clothes rather old-fashioned in style. Why hadn't he noticed them before? The woman seemed so familiar.

By now the sun was setting, and for a while he was blinded by its glare. The two figures were walking away from him toward the poplar trees, and Yann knew he must speak to them. He called out. The man, stopping, waved. Yann heard him say quite clearly, "Son, we are birds, we are free."

Yann ran toward them then, yearning to hear more. They waited, shimmering mirages. All golden they stood, hand in hand. In that moment the sun blinded him again. He blinked, and they were gone.

Looking back the way he had come, he could see where the corn had bowed under his weight. There were no tracks other than his. He lay down, exhausted, and it came to him that the man had spoken Romany. He was reminded of Têtu's story of his mother and her bridegroom, of their wedding the day the soldiers came.

He woke feeling as if he must have been asleep for days, although it was still light, a perfect summer's evening. Thinking back to the couple in the cornfield, he decided they were nothing more than a dream. Now there was peace within him, as if a tempest had passed. All the anger gone, still he asked himself: Can I forgive Têtu?

In the fading light he came to a graveyard and realized, to his surprise, that he had been there before. This was, if he was not mistaken, the Duc de Bourcy's land. Curious as well as hungry, he wondered whether in his disheveled state he could show himself.

Then the thought of seeing the duchess, of explaining, the thought of talking, of being civil, made his hunger seem less important.

He was turning back toward the woods when he glimpsed a light spilling from the kitchen door. He went closer.

On a bench outside sat an old man and a young woman whom Yann recognized as the children's nurse. The small table in front of them was spread with peas that they were busily podding into a copper pan.

He debated with himself what to do, knowing that it was only hunger making him linger, when he heard the girl say, "What do you think will become of our mistress?"

The old man looked despondent. Yann knew what he was thinking: Unless they did something the duchess would be sent to Paris and the guillotine.

Yann came out of the shadows. The old man grabbed hold of the hunting gun resting beside him.

"Please, I mean you no harm." Yann held out his hands. "I am unarmed."

"Are you a deserter from the army?"

"No."

"Are you a priest?"

"No. I came here in March, about two months ago, to help the duke escape to England. Please put the gun down."

The young woman looked at him. "I remember him, Grandpa. He came with the big man. Are you all right, monsieur?"

"Yes. I have been walking. I came this way by chance. I am sorry to have frightened you. I was wondering if your mistress was at home."

The old man still looked uncertain.

"There could be another man with him, Marie. This could be a trap."

"I assure you it isn't."

Reluctantly the old man said, "We'd better go inside the château."

The kitchen was neat and the table well scrubbed. In the light of the oil lamps, Yann caught sight of his reflection in the window and was shocked to see what a wild man of the woods he had become.

The old man, looking at him, said suspiciously, "Are you sure this is the same man? I don't remember him. He looks like a vagabond to me. He smells of woodsmoke."

"It's his eyes," said Marie. "I've never seen eyes like his."

"When I was here there was an attempt to rob the duke, and a man died," said Yann, to put the old man at his ease.

The old man let out a sigh as if he had been holding his breath all this while. "I remember you now. You all went down to the dovecote. The duchess ordered breakfast, but you just wanted a fast horse."

"Correct."

"Monsieur, forgive me. I owe you an apology. I have grown too fearful of late that we will be attacked. My name is Tarlepied. Are you hungry?"

"Ravenous."

Marie, now busy at the stove, said, "Sit, please, and I will make you something to eat."

"These are dreadful days indeed," said the old man. "Farms are going to ruin; the land worked by people who know nothing of the soil, only politics. Fine words don't grow into corn."

"Has the National Guard been here?" Yann asked, remembering the sea of furniture.

"No, monsieur, so far they have left us in peace. Everyone in the village is loyal to the de Bourcy family. The peasants here were all well looked after by the duke. There is a growing resentment about the lack of food, the abolition of the church. Many harbor a secret longing for the old regime."

"Where is your mistress?"

Monsieur Tarlepied said nothing.

Marie looked at him. "Grandpa, we should tell him."

"It goes against the grain . . . but the duke would never forgive me . . ." He sighed. "Ten days ago our mistress left to visit the Marquise de Valory. The duchess was expected to return last week, but today we heard the most terrible news, and I don't know what can be done. One of the Marquise de Valory's servants comes from our village and has been sent back to her family. She is a friend of my granddaughter."

Marie brought an omelet and a bowl of peas to the table. The smell of fresh mint almost overpowered Yann.

"What my friend told me was in confidence, you understand," she said. "But you have helped the family before." She took a deep breath. "She said the Marquis de Valory had been taken to trial, found guilty, and executed. On hearing of it, her mistress went into early labor, and after giving birth became very ill. A few days later the soldiers came to arrest her. She was so poorly. They hid her in the servants' quarters and the duchess pretended to be the Marquise de Valory. She was taken to the prison at Chantilly. She was always a brave woman, my mistress."

"Chantilly," repeated Yann.

"Yes, the château has been made into a prison. Can anything be done?"

"I hope so," said Yann.

That night Yann bathed in a large tin bath and slept in a feather bed. He woke early. Monsieur Tarlepied arrived with breakfast and later shaved Yann, then opened the duke's dressing room for him.

Yann selected a pair of breeches and a waistcoat that belonged to the days of dancing and grand balls, a shirt, and a beautifully embroidered dressing gown, and took them down to the kitchen. He and Marie sat at the table altering the clothes so that the breeches looked like those worn by the National Guard.

By three o'clock, Yann was ready to leave. He stood

at the door dressed in a waistcoat, shirt, breeches and dressing gown, a three-cornered hat with a tricolor pinned to it, and a sash of office across his chest, his boots well worn and muddy.

The old man stared at him, foxed. "Forgive me, monsieur," he said, "but I can't see how this is going to work. You look too eccentric."

Yann lifted his shoulders back, stuck his chest out like a cockerel, and in the thickest of Marseilles accents, which Monsieur Tarlepied could hardly understand, demanded to know why he addressed him as *monsieur*. Wasn't he a patriot?

Marie, looking terrified at the transformation in Yann, backed away. "Stop it, sir, you're frightening us."

"Good," said Yann, "that's the effect I want to achieve. As for the clothes, I will explain that the waistcoat and the dressing gown have come from the Conciergerie, property of a prisoner who was guillotined, a reminder, if one was needed, of what we are fighting for: the freedom of this great country against the tyrannical claw of the past that all this brocade represents."

It was late afternoon when Yann set off, riding the duke's only remaining horse, a fine white stallion that had been loose in the fields and near gone wild. Yann whistled him to come, spoke Romany into his soft ears, and the great horse stood quietly as Yann mounted. Like Yann, he had need of the wind beneath his hooves. Yann's unanswered question came back to him: Should I forgive Têtu? And he was surprised by his own answer.

Yes.

Chapter Eighteen

The grand château of Chantilly purported to be one of the finest specimens of Renaissance architecture. In the moonlight it looked like an enchanted castle, surrounded on all sides by a silvery moat, but its wrought-iron gates had been boarded up to stop any prisoner talking to the outside world. Yann arrived as he had planned, at midnight.

Throughout the journey he had thought about how he was going to free the duchess. He planned to use his new trick, one Têtu had taught him. Yann had spent months perfecting it.

Now that he was here, he realized that only audacity would save him. He started shouting at the top of his lungs.

The old turnkey, gnarled like applewood and pickled in cider, came running, woken from a drunkard's dream. With great effort he pushed the gate open far enough to see who was causing such a rumpus. What the turnkey saw, or thought he saw, standing at the gate were several young men on horseback, all rather oddly dressed.

"I am here from Paris. Take me to the governor. What's wrong with you, man? Stand straight when you talk to me."

Yann handed him a letter, knowing the man couldn't read, which made him considerably easier to deal with.

The turnkey saw on the paper a lot of squiggly lines that looked like the kind of official squiggly lines one might need to see the prison governor.

The gate ground open all the way and Yann was in.

"My horse needs feeding and watering. Did you hear me? Jump to it!"

Yann's voice was very loud, loud enough to waken the dead. It worked. Lights appeared at windows. Half-dressed, the guards came running.

"I want to see the governor of the prison now," he demanded.

He was taken to see Citizen Notte.

The prison governor came reluctantly from his bedchamber, wearing a dressing gown quite inferior to the one worn by this very handsome and assured young man.

Yann handed him the papers. He examined them carefully, and all the while Yann's eyes never left him.

Citizen Notte put them down. "All seems aboveboard. Just the one prisoner, I see."

"That is correct."

The governor was staring at Yann. "What is your name?"

"Socrates," Yann replied.

"And what was it, citizen, before this new fashion to have Greek names?"

"The name of a saint that stinks of the old regime."

Citizen Notte could see this earnest young man took his job very seriously indeed, and without an ounce of humor to lighten his load.

"Quite. Will you be wanting a bed for the night?"

"The public prosecutor's office never sleeps. This woman is wanted in court tomorrow in Paris. My duty is to get her there. I shall need a carriage."

This came as a real blow. Carriages were valuable and scarce.

"You mean you didn't bring one?" said Citizen Notte, beginning to wake up. "We are very short of such things. A farm cart, maybe?"

"No, it wouldn't get there fast enough."

"I should tell you that we are understaffed. I suppose you will need a prison guard to accompany you as well?"

"Why? She is just one miserable woman."

There was a knock on the door and a man entered. His eyes, too wide apart, had the look of a zealot, burning with fanatical passion. It was clear that mercy was not high on his list of priorities.

"This is my right-hand man, Citizen Marchand of the Revolutionary Army."

Yann had seen his name in secret reports that Cordell had shown him. He knew that Marchand worked in confidence for the Committee of Public Safety and his ambition was to be transferred to Paris to work with Robespierre. Yann was more wary of Citizen Marchand than he was of the governor. For a start, he was stone-cold sober. And he took the papers from Citizen Notte before Yann had had a chance to work on him.

"What are these?" he demanded. "There's nothing written here. What's your game? Who are you?"

Yann puffed himself up like a great cockerel. "I am here on business for the public prosecutor's office."

He spoke slowly, concentrating on getting a hold on Marchand's mind.

Citizen Notte looked flustered and took back the papers to study them again. Visible relief spread over his face as he handed them to Yann.

"I hope there's nothing wrong with your eyes, citizen, for this is all correct. I am about to give orders for the woman to be brought down to the courtyard."

Marchand snatched the papers from Yann and saw quite clearly the name of the prisoner. He looked momentarily uncertain; and yet there could be no denying this letter was from Fouquier-Tinville's office.

Yann could see how he was battling with his reason, as if doubt still threatened to get the better of him.

"Strange," he murmured.

Yann knew he had him.

"No, what's strange, citizen, is that you questioned my word. I think certain friends at the Hôtel de Ville should know that."

"I meant no offense," said Marchand.

"Just get me the prisoner. I haven't got all night for these bourgeois pleasantries."

Citizen Notte looked genuinely worried as he rang the bell, longing for this to be over, and for the young man and his prisoner to be gone.

A guard entered and spoke to Citizen Notte in a whisper.

"What is it?" said Marchand.

"There is a problem. The prisoner says she won't leave without the young girl who is sharing her cell."

He looked at Yann, who knew exactly what he was expected to say: that they were to drag her out by her hair if necessary, he cared nothing for any attachment the traitor might have formed.

Instead he said, "How old is she, citizen?"

The governor looked at the list. "She is sixteen, sir. The whole family was arrested for hiding a priest. Her parents and older brother were guillotined last week."

"Sounds to me as if she's guilty as hell. Better bring her along. They like all different ages on the scaffold."

Ten minutes later a battered old carriage that looked and smelled as if it had been used as a henhouse was pulled into the courtyard, together with a tired-looking horse. Keeping his head low, Yann opened the carriage door to make sure he had the right prisoners.

"What's this?" shouted Yann, seeing the horse. "This

213

nag's good for nothing but glue! I have to be in Paris by the morning, not next week."

There was a panic among the guards. Marchand suggested he should use his own horse.

"What?" said Yann. "My horse is employed by the Republic to take me wherever I'm needed. It's not meant for pulling henhouses."

Reluctantly Marchand led out a fine dapple gray.

"It's mine, I—"

Yann interrupted. "What's yours is mine, citizen. Remember we are all one now."

He waited as the old horse was unharnessed and Marchand's gray put in its place, then climbed up and took the reins. He had set off toward the gates with the duke's horse tied to the back of the rickety vehicle when he heard Marchand call.

"Wait!"

Yann's heart sank. He could see the open road. He could smell freedom. He was so nearly there. He had a mad impulse to make a dash for it, to get away. That, he knew, would be suicide.

Marchand ran up to him. "You will put in a good word for me?" he said. "I am hoping to be transferred to Paris."

"Again you waste my valuable time. Good morning to you, citizen," said Yann, and he cracked his whip and set off.

The day had dawned by the time they came to a crossroads in the forest. He took the carriage down an overgrown path as far as he could so that they were well hidden.

He opened the carriage door. The interior was coated with feathers, and perched on one of the upholstered seats was a hen that had obstinately refused to leave. The duchess sat in the opposite corner, the girl fast asleep, resting her head on her shoulder. Both had had their hair cut off so that what was left stuck up in tufts.

The hen seemed the most vocal of the three occupants. Yann grabbed it.

"May I ask why we have stopped?" said the duchess, only glancing at her jailer. She was painfully thin.

"Maybe I wanted an egg for breakfast," Yann said kindly. Still she refused to look at him.

The girl woke, sleepily taking in this apparition. Before her was a handsome young man, extraordinarily dressed, with a hen under his arm.

"Are you going to kill it?"

Yann studied the hen. "No," he said. "It looks like a

good layer." And he went off to put it in his saddlebag.

The two women climbed uncertainly out of the carriage. The duchess looked around, wondering if this was going to be her end, to be slaughtered here in this wood. Seeing the girl was terrified, she said calmly, "It is all right, Celeste."

Yann came back with bread and a bottle of wine.

"This is for you, madame. Do you not recognize me?"

The duchess finally looked at him. Catching the smile in his dark eyes, her face lit up with joy. "Tell me I am not dreaming!"

She put her arms around the girl. "There is no need to be frightened. This young gentleman is an old friend of mine."

Yann bowed.

And the girl, looking at him, said, "Does that mean we are saved?"

Chapter Nineteen

Yann arrived in Paris the day before *The Harlequinade* was due to reopen. He'd gone straight to the Hôtel de Ville. There was one more thing he had to do.

The clerk whose business it was to draw up the names of the guillotined had had a busy morning. The previous day there had been a record harvest of heads, and in the enthusiasm to rid France of traitors and aristocrats, names had become muddled. Now, his finger black with ink, he looked up wearily at the sans-culotte before him.

"Where are the documents?"

He peered over his smudged glasses and added three more names to the list, a thin smile curling like smoke across his face. Head bowed, tongue protruding, he wrote down the names, each one gloriously misspelled.

Yann only bothered to correct him on one: the Duchesse de Bourcy. Her best chance of survival was to be dead to the authorities. The clerk dusted the ink and handed the paper to an officer to be posted outside.

"Good work, citizen," said the clerk.

Only when that was done did Yann return to the Circus of Follies.

Citizeness Manou, seeing a sans-culotte with a three-cornered hat at the stage door, emerged from her sentry box in a cloud of smoky thunder and was taken aback to realize it was none other than Yann.

"Citizen Aulard is waiting in his office, and I'm under strict instructions to send you up the minute I see you."

Yann climbed the stairs to Citizen Aulard's office to find the theater manager, Têtu, and a young man he had never seen before. He was a year or two older than himself, had dark blond hair and a pleasing, handsome face, though Yann thought he looked as if he hadn't slept for days.

"There you are," said Citizen Aulard as Yann entered

the room. "Thank the Lord above, you're back. *The Harlequinade* opens tomorrow."

"I know that," said Yann.

Têtu knew from one look at Yann that he was, in part, forgiven.

"This is the Vicomte de Reignac," he said. "He was about to tell us how he came here. Please continue, Viscount."

"Wait," Yann interrupted. "Surely you were sent to us?"

"No," said Têtu, "the viscount came to us through an unusual channel."

"Yes, the priest who was hiding me made inquiries as to the whereabouts of the Silver Blade, and was told they might know of him at the Circus of Follies," said the viscount.

"That's the part I don't like," said Citizen Aulard. "Not one little bit."

"It's not important," said Yann, recognizing in this young man a sadness all too familiar, one he had seen so often in those who had lost loved ones. So much heartbreak. Paris was broken by grief.

The Vicomte de Reignac spoke quietly with a slight stammer. He had lost his father, his mother, and his beloved fifteen-year-old sister. His father and sister had been taken to the guillotine three days previously.

"My mother and I escaped arrest. She insisted on going to the Place de la Révolution to be near them. I tried to stop her, but nothing would hold her back. She wanted to get as close to the tumbrel as she could to touch the hem of my sister's dress."

He stopped, fighting back tears.

"I watched my sister go up to the scaffold. One of the executioner's assistants pulled off the cap she wore, and she flinched with the pain. They had cut off her long blond hair. My mother let out a gasp and my sister, looking frantically into the crowd, called '*Maman!*' I knew there was nothing that could be done. I begged my mother to be quiet, but she was inconsolable. When my father went to the guillotine, she rushed toward the scaffold. I tried to stop her, but was held back by a man in the crowd. He said, 'Monsieur, if you do anything, you too will be caught. Get out of here while you can.' I took no notice, but tried to get free. Again this stranger restrained me."

"Who was he?" asked Têtu.

"I found out that he had known my parents. He was a priest who had taken Holy Communion with them and had listened to their confessions."

"What happened next?" asked Citizen Aulard.

"They sentenced my mother then and there, without the inconvenience of a trial, for showing emotion for a traitor to liberty. They bound her hands, they cut off her hair. She looked almost happy. I think it was that that riled them. They tied her to the plank and then lifted the blade of the guillotine, leaving it suspended. The blood of my sister and my father fell like rain upon her and the crowd shouted abuse."

He stopped, wiped his eyes, and took a shuddering breath.

"After an hour, mercifully, the blade fell. I was saved that day by the priest. He hid me and told me about the legend of the Silver Blade. I can't stay with him; it's too dangerous. I need to get out of France."

Citizen Aulard was shaken. "What has happened? When did people become this cruel?"

"When Pandora opened her box," said Têtu.

Yann put a hand on the young man's shoulder. "You will be leaving very soon. You must rest now."

"Thank you," said the Vicomte de Reignac. "May I ask when I will meet the Silver Blade?"

"You have met him."

Têtu followed Yann outside and asked, "Are you

mad? That was unwise, telling him who you are. Supposing—"

"Têtu," said Yann, "I am not sure *who* I am. Why shouldn't I be the Silver Blade? If I were you, I would say nothing more on the subject."

Têtu sighed and shrugged his shoulders.

At the stage door Citizeness Manou said, "Have you heard about Colombine, then?"

"No," said Yann, stopping.

"She is now Citizeness Loup. Got married two days ago. Ah, they make a fine couple, but mind you, I don't call it proper. I mean, it wasn't done in a church, and in my humble opinion, that doesn't count. Still, he looks like an angel, lucky girl."

"Looks can be deceptive," said Yann.

Colombine turned up for rehearsal that afternoon.

"I hear congratulations are in order," said Yann.

"Yes. Thanks," she said, her voice sounding strained.

"It was very sudden."

Colombine did her best to avoid looking at Yann. "I suppose so," she said.

"Are you all right?"

"Of course. Never happier."

222

"Good. Well, I wish you both the best."

"Thanks," she said again, eager to be gone.

Pantalon came rushing up and caught Colombine by the arm. Yann noticed her wince.

"Pardon," said Pantalon, "I haven't hurt you, have I?"

"No, no."

"Good. There is an hour of bliss before the curtain rises. Who wishes to join me at the café on the corner? Colombine, come on, let me buy you a drink."

She glanced toward the stage door. "I think I will rest, if you don't mind."

Pantalon watched her leave and, turning to Yann, shrugged. "She's not herself. Have you noticed that?"

At the opening performance of *The Harlequinade,* the viscount appeared as an extra on the stage, for as Têtu had predicted, the police decided to pay the newly opened theater a visit.

The viscount was dressed as a young woman and looked every inch the part. Two of the gendarmerie stood watching from the wings, quite enchanted, blowing kisses and acting the fool until they were called away, neither knowing that they had been watching the very man they were searching for.

Afterward, Yann sat in his dressing room removing his makeup, pleased to have gotten through the show. But his thoughts were interrupted by the sound of raised voices. It appeared to be an argument between Colombine and her new husband. Quite what was being said Yann wasn't sure, although Colombine's voice grew shriller until it became a cry as something fell on the floor with a deafening thud.

Yann got up and went along the corridor to Colombine's dressing room. Without knocking, he went in, to see her crumpled in the corner, and Anselm standing over her.

"Get out," said Anselm. "This is between me and her. Get out. It doesn't concern you."

Yann pinned him against the wall. "Calm down. That is no way to treat your wife."

"I can do what I bloody well please. She needs to learn some manners."

"If you hit her again while you are in this theater, you will answer to me. Do you understand?"

Yann let go of Anselm, wondering why it was he couldn't read this rat of a man's thoughts. It was as if somehow they'd been interfered with.

As he turned to help Colombine to her feet, Anselm lifted a chair.

Colombine tried to find her voice to warn Yann as it came hurtling down toward him, but the chair stopped short an inch from its target. Yann, without even turning around, clicked his fingers and sent it back the way it had come with such force that it smashed to pieces on Anselm's blond, cherub-like curls.

"I will kill you," shouted Anselm, pulling a knife.

Making a dash toward Yann, he found that his feet were no longer on the ground. Instead he was hanging upside down, spinning like a child's top. He dropped the knife, which hung, caught in midair.

Citizeness Manou came to see what the commotion was about. As she helped Colombine from the room, Yann clicked his fingers again and Anselm fell, unconscious, to the floor.

Later that night, numbing his rage with cheap wine, his sides hurting, his head reeling, Anselm was aware of an unstoppable force entering the bar. Milkeye gripped him by the collar and dragged him to the Place de la Révolution. Only there did he let him go and, looking up, Anselm found himself face-to-face with Count Kalliovski. Balthazar was at his side.

"You have let me down," said Kalliovski, his voice razor-sharp. Balthazar growled.

"I can get the information. I can. I mean, I know that Yann Margoza works at the theater and that the dwarf Têtu is there—"

"You're not very clever, are you? Do you think I don't know all that and more? What I needed was for you to become a part of the company, for the actress Colombine to feel that you would never betray her. Instead you beat your new wife."

"I can do it."

"You are nothing more than a common thug, a pretty bully boy. You bore me. All your kind bore me." Kalliovski pushed his index finger into Anselm's cheek. For a moment he felt that his face was on fire.

"I can get her back. I can, honest I can. I know how and—"

Kalliovski's laughter resounded around the Place de la Révolution. "What you know about women is nothing. You are ignorant. You are a slug, a miserable, slimy slug. What, I wonder, did I see in you?" Kalliovski began to walk away.

"I will do anything, master, please!" shouted Anselm. "Anything! Give me another chance!"

Kalliovski turned. "You have a week. If you fail . . . I need another chandelier, and your bones will fit my design beautifully. Or perhaps another talking head would be amusing. I haven't yet decided. Fail me, and you are dead. I have no mercy."

Anselm shivered as he watched them all disappear into the night. Breathing heavily, he leaned against the winding cloth of the guillotine, relieved still to be alive. Something brushed against his legs and he stood suddenly upright, the hairs on the back of his neck prickling.

He looked down to see rats, black as the plague, scuttling from under the scaffold, running between his legs, over his shoes. A soundless scream, bone-hard, caught in his throat. Terrified, he scurried away. The lugubrious shadow of the guillotine followed him.

At the theater, Yann was still in his dressing room when Didier knocked on the door.

"I've been sent to fetch you. There's a real rumbus going on in the office. Cordell is here."

"Wait, Didier," said Yann, "is there any news about Remon Quint?"

"None. I went down to the catacombs while you were away, but I couldn't find that passage again. What do you think happened to him?"

"I don't know." Yann sighed. "But he had the smell of death upon him."

"Is that another Gypsy superstition?"

"I felt it the moment I first saw him. It never got any better."

Didier shook his head. "It's a bad business, that's for sure."

"Where the devil have you been?" said Cordell when Yann walked into the office.

"Downstairs."

"No, I mean for the past week. What have you been doing?"

"Walking."

"What were you thinking? It was no time to take a grand tour, with Remon Quint missing. You were needed here, to help sort out this mess. And if you had been here, we might have been able to save the Duchesse de Bourcy from the guillotine. But you weren't— you were rambling about the countryside. It's too late now. She and her friend the Marquise de Valory were both executed yesterday, along with Madame Picard's daughter Celeste, who was only fifteen years old."

"Sixteen," said Yann, "and I am glad to hear it."

Cordell hit the desk. "That's preposterous, sir! What is wrong with you? Glad to hear it? Have you lost your mind?"

"No," said Yann, "but now that they are all dead, they might be able to live in relative peace."

Cordell looked at Têtu and Citizen Aulard. His temper had suddenly evaporated. Yann was ill; that could be the only explanation.

"Maybe you've had too much sun. God knows what I'll write to the duke. I gave him my word I would protect her."

"Then tell him that his wife is in excellent health," said Yann, "that she suffered her ordeal with great courage. The only damage done is to her hair, which was cut off. And that the girl Celeste who shared the duchess's cell is a delight, and thrilled to have exchanged a prison cell for the de Bourcy château. And no, I haven't lost my mind."

Cordell's face was grave. "Yann, I have the official reports. Do you wish to see them? They were all executed."

"No, I've seen them already. After all, I wrote them."

There was silence. Then Citizen Aulard burst out laughing. Cordell looked completely stunned. A smile crossed Têtu's face.

"I came home past the Hôtel de Ville and they were very grateful to know that three more traitors had been sacrificed at the bloody altar. I made sure their names were posted. The governor of the prison at Chantilly will confirm that two of his prisoners were sent to the guillotine."

"I think," said Cordell quietly, "I owe you an apology."

"You owe me nothing," said Yann. "Write to the duke and tell him there is life after death."

Chapter Twenty

Auguste, Viscomte de Reignac, first met Sido de Villeduval at a summer ball. His arrival in London caused no end of a stir among the émigré society, for Auguste de Reignac belonged to that rare breed of aristocrats who not only held a bona fide title but, more remarkable still, had managed to escape France with their fortune intact.

Juliette had been delighted to see the effect her niece had on this handsome, shy young man. Her beauty had already attracted many admirers, who treated her as if she were made of porcelain, a precious object to be treasured, worshipped.

Sido had the feeling that she was nothing more than a pencil sketch to be filled in and colored to suit the needs of others, to be adored by the foppish young dandies who treated her like a lame Madonna. At balls, she was left to sit with whining, horse-faced ladies, whose dance cards were empty, and listen while their vicious tongues sliced and cut their prettier sisters.

Auguste de Reignac was different. He sat beside her and engaged her in intelligent conversation. He told her of his flight from Paris and how with the help of a young man named Yann Margoza, he'd escaped. As he talked, he noticed Sido's eyes brighten to a radiant blue.

"Yann," she said, "rescued me from Paris as well, at the beginning of the September Massacre."

"Of course, forgive me. I didn't make the connection. Your father was the Marquis de Villeduval?"

"That is correct."

"What a terrible ordeal you must have suffered. I heard that the marquis was killed. Perhaps it was a mercy his mind had gone. I hope he was unaware of what was happening."

"I pray so," said Sido. "And I heard about your family too. I am sorry."

"I have decided to live," said Auguste seriously. "I think I must, as I have no idea why it should be me that is here, not my sister or . . ." He stopped, the subject too painful for this garish ballroom. "Would you kindly do me the honor of dancing with me?"

And Sido, who had too long waited for someone to ask her, didn't hesitate to say yes.

That evening there were many frustrated young beaux who realized they'd missed a golden opportunity with the beautiful Marquise de Villeduval, who danced delightfully, with an elegance of movement and an energy that lit up the room.

Going home in the carriage, Juliette had been quietly thrilled with Sido, and felt that at last Yann Margoza would be replaced in her affections by this altogether more suitable young man.

The next day Juliette invited Auguste to dine.

The drawing room at Queen Square that evening was full, as it often was, with émigrés newly arrived in London, and others who had been in exile far longer and were now beginning to wonder if they would ever be able to return home.

As soon as Juliette was engrossed in conversation with the Duc de Bourcy, Sido asked Auguste to tell her more about his escape.

"We went out of Paris through the catacombs. Yann took me all the way to Le Havre and didn't leave until he was certain I was safe," Auguste said. "Have you ever seen him perform on stage?"

"Once, when I was younger. He was a magician's assistant then. Have you?"

"I was on stage at the Circus of Follies. I took the role of a market seller. Harlequin came on, upset the stall to a great deal of laughter, and then without touching anything—and I mean anything—he put each and every piece back on the stall. I was told to stay silent, whatever I did, but that if he asked a question I was to move my mouth. I did, and—this is the oddest part—out of it came words as if I were speaking, though I said nothing."

Auguste de Reignac had gone home that evening full of fine food and wine, and in love with the most enchanting pair of blue eyes.

The day after the supper party, Sido received a letter from Yann, and nothing could have prepared her for what he had to say. She opened it, disappointed to find only one sheet, and with so few words. Not suspecting anything to be wrong, she read:

Dear Sido:

Please forgive me for taking so long to write to you. What I have to tell you I say with a heavy heart.

Sido, we can never be together. It is and always has been an impossible situation, a dream. It would take more than a revolution before a marquis's daughter and a Gypsy would be allowed to marry. For that is my origin, as I am certain by now you will have been told.

Please burn my letters. If you remember me at all, I hope it will be with affection. We will never meet again, and I wish you all the happiness in the world.

You deserve a better man than me.

Once again, I ask you to forgive me for any injury I may have caused you.

Do not dwell on the past. Live for the future.

Yann

Sido couldn't breathe. She read the letter again, the room spinning, the world disintegrating under her feet. Could love just vanish? One day it was everything, the next gone, like a passing fever? Was that how love took men?

Her knees gave way and she crumpled to the floor. His words were stones in her heart.

Oh Lord, don't let our love turn to ashes. Don't let it be an illusion. Yann is my rock, my strength, he gives meaning to my life. To him I'm not just a puppet made to dance for the delight of others. His love makes me whole. His love makes me free . . . His love . . . I thought he loved me.

How often have I dreamed of us living far away where no one would know our history, no one would judge us? Of Yann sitting with our children in front of the fire, telling them a fairy tale of how his magic saved their mama from the wicked Count Kalliovski, how he smuggled her out of a gated city. We would have grown old together . . .

Like the broken banks of a river in flood, she felt her soul swept away by grief. She sat hunched on the floor, her arms wrapped around her body, rocking with pain. She could hear voices downstairs, the clocks in the hall ticking, outside a street seller shouting his wares, and another sound, the echo of unbearable loneliness that stretched before her for all eternity. Her trembling hands took the talisman from around her neck. Now there was nothing to protect her. She wrote:

It is returned safely to you, but you still have my heart and my soul.

That afternoon Sido went to see Mr. Trippen, taking her letter with her. From the drawing room window Juliette watched her get into a sedan chair and vaguely noticed a man in a three-cornered hat setting off after it.

Juliette had for weeks tried to persuade Henry that Sido's English lessons with Mr. Trippen should stop, that he couldn't be trusted, not after his irresponsible behavior regarding the letters.

"Fiddlesticks," Henry had said. "A load of tosh, and, my dear, you know it. It does the girl good to have a change of scenery. Besides, her English is much improved. The lessons will continue."

"And the letters?" Juliette had added.

"Leave that to me."

Henry had said nothing to Mr. Trippen on the matter, and the letters had gone back and forth between the two lovers without any more interruption.

Now Mr. Trippen stood by the empty fireplace in his battered housecoat and red hat with a tassel, and read the letter Sido had shown him.

"I don't know what to do," she said.

"My dear enchanting lady," said Mr. Trippen, "tell

me you have done nothing reckless. The seas of emotion can so capsize young love."

"I want to send back the talisman, you know, the shell Yann gave me. I have wrapped it up and—"

"I think that is most unwise," said Mr. Trippen.

Sido knew it was, but if Yann loved her no more, then in all truth she couldn't wear it. Tears threatened to overcome her. She said, as lightly as her voice would allow, "That's because you are an old sentimentalist."

"No, it is because it is a very important talisman. As to this letter, Hamlet's lines do not ring true. He has not stopped loving you, and the fact he is a Gypsy would never have deterred either of you from being together. Or would it?" he said, looking at Sido's pale face.

"No."

"Trippen smells something rotten in the state of Denmark and you, my dear, are to be no Ophelia. That way madness lies. In my humble but well-considered opinion, something dark is troubling our Hamlet. The question—and the question is always king, my dear—is what is it that he is not saying?"

Sido's thoughts that rainy day were in turmoil as the sedan chair took her back to Queen Square. How, she wondered, shall I cope with a broken heart? How shall I manage when my soul is dying? All she wanted to do was lie in a corner, curled up like a cat, and let time roll over her, instead of which she had to find the strength to hide her feelings. What could she do now? All she possessed was a title. She had no money, and she couldn't go on living with her aunt and uncle indefinitely. Perhaps she could be a governess? Oh, dear God, there were already enough French women of noble birth in her position, who were now obliged to earn their livings. The newspapers were filled with advertisements.

Or she could marry. She knew that if she wasn't betrothed by the end of this season, her aunt would be bitterly disappointed. Juliette was certain that Auguste would soon ask for her hand in marriage. Could she do that? Marry a man she didn't love, for grand carriages and pretty dresses, for security against poverty? Many a young woman would tell her she was greatly privileged to have the chance. For Auguste was gentle, kind—and not elderly. Still, without love, it made everything a folly. She would never make him happy, and she knew she would never love him as she loved Yann.

That evening at supper she listened to her aunt discourse endlessly about the merits of marriage and the finer details of the Viscomte de Reignac's fortune. Sido noticed that Henry, like her, was silent on the matter.

The next day Auguste came on the pretext of bringing Sido a book by Burke, *Reflections on the Revolution in France*.

"I thought you would be interested in it," he said as they sat in the drawing room.

"We are planning a picnic on Hampstead Heath for the day after tomorrow if the weather holds," Juliette said. "We would be delighted to have your company."

"Alas, madame, I cannot. I am leaving London."

"Where are you going?"

"To America."

"But that is so far away."

"I agree, but I own land in Boston and need to see that my interests are secure. I can assure you, I shall be back here soon. In fact, nothing would keep me away."

Sido felt a rising sense of panic as she saw her aunt get up to leave.

"Where are you going, Aunt?" she said, a little too urgently.

"I am sure, my dear, that you two have quite enough to talk about without my company. Viscount, shall I order some tea for you?"

———

Alone in the drawing room with the ticking clocks, Sido, terrified that Auguste was going to propose, said quickly, "Don't, we are such good friends, and . . ."

"I—I insist," he stammered. "I know you don't love me, but I am in love with you and I want you to be my wife. It would be enough just to have you with me."

"No—oh, you deserve so much more than that. You must find love."

He took Sido's hand. "I would settle for your companionship, for your wit and intelligence. I would be happy."

"No, no," said Sido. "What about passion? Surely there must be passion?"

"It is a fleeting thing. I could live without it, and perhaps—in time . . . you would come to love me."

She turned away. "I couldn't live without passion. It's what makes us soar. And I refuse to think of you not finding that in your life." She laughed. "I tell you, when you do, you will wonder how we could ever have had this conversation."

He took her hand. "Please don't say no. Don't turn me away. Think about my proposal. I sail in two days, and I'm willing to wait until my return."

"No . . . I love . . ." She stopped.

"Yann Margoza," he said slowly.

"How do you know?"

"I would be a fool not to see it, the way your eyes light up when we talk of him. So tell me—is there any hope? Or am I just dreaming with my eyes open?"

"I like you very much as a friend."

"Then that is a start, some would say a good start."

"I know I would never make you happy, and you who have been through such pain deserve to be loved, and I am certain that you will find it."

Auguste took her hand and kissed it. "Then, *ma chère* marquise, say no more, I understand. After all, I owe Yann my life. He is a lucky man to have won your heart. I will always be your friend. I hope our friendship, at least, may continue?"

"Yes, by all means, yes."

"You have chosen a very fine man indeed. I hope he realizes how fortunate he is."

She watched him go, heard the front door click shut, and saw Juliette standing in the hall, a look of disbelief on her face.

———

Two days later Auguste de Reignac sailed for America, by which time Juliette could hardly bring herself to speak to Sido, so furious was she that her niece should willfully turn down a proposal of marriage—a proposal that would have set her up as a woman of means with property in France and America.

Again Henry regretted he had not told Juliette the truth about Yann, but now was not the time. The situation in Paris was deteriorating, and he had received a report from Cordell confirming the truth of the unwelcome rumor that Count Kalliovski appeared to be alive and active. Henry, sitting in his office looking out over the square, was grateful for one thing: Sido was safe in London.

Chapter Twenty-one

It happened just as Sido was leaving Mr. Trippen's house in Maiden Lane. The maid, Betsy, had her hand on the latch of the front door when Mr. Trippen called from the landing.

"Wait, dear girl, before you go. You nearly forgot this." And he held out the talisman.

"I thought," said Sido, "you had sent it back to Yann as I asked."

"No. I think he wouldn't want that. You must keep it safely on you." He opened the catch and gently hung it around her neck.

Afterward he was pleased he'd done it. In fact it was the only thing that brought him any comfort. For when Betsy did open the door, two armed men were standing there with handkerchiefs concealing their faces and their hats pulled down. Behind them the sedan chair lay on its side with the Laxtons' two footmen out cold.

One thug grabbed Sido by the arm, and Mr. Trippen, without thinking, went into battle. He heard a loud bang, smelled burning flesh and thought nothing of it.

"Let her go! Take your hands off her!"

Sido was lifted bodily and carried away. Mr. Trippen, by now feeling as if he were made of air rather than flesh and blood, fell to the ground.

Betsy watched, ashen faced and stone-statue-still, as Sido was dragged down Maiden Lane to where a very smart carriage stood, its windows blacked out. She saw Sido bundled into it and then the carriage disappeared from view.

All Sido could think of as the carriage drove off at speed was that her abductors had killed Mr. Trippen. As she tried in the dark to open the door, she became aware of someone sitting on the seat opposite. Only when the man lit his clay pipe, the flame illuminating his face, did she recognize him.

"You've got more spark about you than I expected," said Mr. Tull.

"You have killed Mr. Trippen."

"The old fool should have minded his own business instead of acting the hero." Mr. Tull laughed. "As for you, if you don't do as you're told, miss, you'll end up as dead meat. Do I make myself quite clear?"

It was early evening when they came to the courtyard of The Travelers' Arms. It was busy, and the arrival of one more coach, even with blackened windows, went almost unnoticed. Sido was bundled up the wooden steps that led to a gantry off which Mr. Tull had arranged for two rooms. He locked Sido in the first room while he went to see about food, for Mr. Tull was ruled by the needs of his stomach.

Sido looked hopelessly at the miserable furnishings: ponderous chairs and a small robust desk. Bored travelers, no doubt waiting for the packet to France, had carved their names into its surface. She turned the key, not expecting any good fortune, but found there a pot of nearly dried ink, some broken quills, and a few sheets of clean paper. It struck her that this was her last opportunity to tell anyone what had befallen her. The nibs and the thickness of the ink made writing difficult.

I am alive. I am at an inn near the coast and fear I am to be to returned to France. Mr. Tull kidnapped me, his man shot Mr. Trippen.

She addressed it to Mr. Laxton and propped it behind a painting of a galleon at sea, which hung on the wall above the desk. She wished she had said more, but her reason was so clouded by the fear of being caught, she could hardly think straight. To her horror, she noticed an ink stain on her finger, and hurriedly licked and rubbed at it until the stain looked as if it had been there for some time. She had managed to lock the desk and to slip the key through a crack in the floorboards when she heard the door being unlocked. Mr. Tull came in, a napkin tied around his neck, his mouth full. He snapped his fingers and two servants dressed in black entered, one carrying a silver goblet.

"Drink this," he said.

"What is it?" demanded Sido, determined to show no fear.

Mr. Tull smiled, or at least that was the impression he gave, though he looked less than pleased to have his order questioned.

"Drink."

"Not unless I know what's in—"

247

Mr. Tull pulled the napkin from around his neck and threw it on the floor in disgust.

"Do as you're told, my girl."

"I insist you tell me what's in it," Sido repeated.

She suddenly felt belligerent, knowing it was her only power, and she refused to let the feeling go. Mr. Tull turned on his heel and left the room. Sido thought for a moment that she might have won, but then he came back carrying a metal funnel.

"Hold her head back," he commanded the servants.

Sido was pushed, fighting, into the armchair. She struggled, biting Mr. Tull hard on the hand. She could taste blood. He hit her across the face and for a moment she blacked out.

"Hold her!"

Sido's jaw was pried open and the funnel pushed down her throat. Gagging but unable to resist, she swallowed the bitter-tasting liquid.

She remembered trying to get up and Mr. Tull shouting, "Give her some more!"

And again she was held down. Then nothing, just a dark abyss.

Chapter Twenty-two

Poor Citizen Aulard found the plays he had been instructed to put on so full of patriotic drivel, they were almost too hard to bear.

"I tell you, Têtu, it was a travesty last night. You should have seen the nonsense. The minute the play started, this man in the audience stood up and said he had written a song and could he sing it. Never have you heard such sentimental rubbish from a Frenchman. After that, what need of the play? Everyone started to sing and shout and march upon the stage like barbarians. I could have wept."

Têtu brought out cheese and a loaf of bread and put them on the theater manager's desk. Citizen Aulard's eyes lit up.

"Hunger, my friend, doesn't help," said Têtu kindly. "What will happen tonight?" he asked, producing two glasses and a bottle of wine.

Citizen Aulard raised his hands in the air. "More of the same," he said, then added, "I have been thinking."

"A dangerous thing, my friend, at a time like this."

"Maybe, but let me tell you: If we survive the Reign of Terror, I don't wish to stay in France. I never thought I would live to say that. Perhaps I've become a Gypsy in my old age. Still, I have a mind to go and take my chances in the New World, in America. There, Têtu, we could put on real magic performances. What I'm proposing is that we should be partners."

Têtu laughed. "Better that you asked me for some Gypsy luck, for that is what you need, not a partner."

Iago squawked. "I've seen you where you never were . . ."

"Quiet!" shouted Citizen Aulard. "That bird is getting on my nerves."

"One day you will be grateful you have a parrot. Anyway, it is a line from a Gypsy poem. Shall I tell you it?" And without waiting for a reply Têtu continued:

"I've seen you where you never were
And where you never be.
And yet within that very place
You can be seen by me.
For to tell what they do not know
Is the art of the Romany."

Citizen Aulard laughed. "I thought I would end my days with a beautiful actress by my side. Instead I find a daft dwarf, who I am too fond of to be parted from."

Têtu smiled. "The New World might well appeal to my restless feet, that is if we get out of this alive, but I am not certain that Yann would want to come."

Citizen Aulard sighed. He had been avoiding this topic of conversation, for something was very wrong with Yann. Gone was his calm good sense, his cool head.

"Explain to me what has happened to him. Ever since we lost Remon Quint, he is a changed man."

"I know," said Têtu.

"I have been told," said Citizen Aulard, "that silver blades are again being found after someone has escaped. It is madness. There is enough talk already. If he goes on like this, he will be . . ." He drew his finger across his neck. "What is he trying to do? Get himself killed and us too in the process?"

Têtu went to the door and looked out.

"What is it?" asked Aulard.

"Nothing. I thought I heard something."

"You see? We are all jumping like circus fleas. Yann must be stopped." Citizen Aulard looked thoughtfully at Têtu.

"I've seen you where you never were . . ." repeated the parrot.

"There is an explanation for Yann's behavior, and I am not sure what to do," said Têtu.

"That is most unlike you."

"Yann has stumbled on a secret that I have done my best to conceal from him, for his own sake."

"Already I don't like the sound of this."

"It is hard to explain, but in our world the spirits play as great a role as the living. Yann's mother, Anis, believed that his spirit father was her lost love, Manouche. She never wanted him to know the identity of his real father."

Citizen Aulard took a sip of wine. "Come, it can't be so terrible—"

"One day I will tell you the whole story," interrupted Têtu. "It is Kalliovski."

Wine sprayed in a fountain from the startled theater manager's mouth. He started coughing.

"Kalliovski? No, no, tell me I have misheard. All the angels in heaven and hell! Tell me I have misheard!"

Outside the door, Anselm shifted in the shadows. He'd come up from the stage door on an errand for Citizeness Manou, eager for any excuse to listen in on the theater manager's conversations. Like a magpie, he collected gems of information and took them back to his master. He listened intently in the dust-filled silence, unable to believe what he was hearing.

Anselm, like many before him, had fallen under the count's spell, and he was sure the dwarf spoke nothing but poisonous lies. It was not possible that Yann Margoza was his master's son. He had convinced himself that he was the rightful heir to the Kalliovski crown.

Anselm walked slowly down the stairs to the stage door. Everything had turned red, vivid, bright red. He wanted to kill someone. It didn't matter whom. Just someone.

"Well," said Citizeness Manou, "what did he say?"

"What?" said Anselm.

"I sent you up there to give Citizen Aulard a message, and you forgot, didn't you?" She shuffled out of her sentry box, wheezing and panting. Pushing past him, she said, "As usual I have to do everything myself round here."

Anselm, lost in a blind fury, didn't answer. He left the theater and, crossing the square, went to the Café du Coin, where he sat shaking with rage, mulling over what he would do. He knew he would only find peace by killing. In the past a chicken would have satisfied him, but not now. Now he needed something more than a scrawny neck.

He saw Citizeness Manou leaving the theater. She stopped to adjust her cap and set off, a long, thin quaff of smoke following her. Anselm felt his fingers tingle. He paid and left.

Walking behind Citizeness Manou, keeping to the shadows, he waited to pounce. Then he saw his opportunity: an alleyway with a dead end, and Citizeness Manou so obligingly stopping at the corner to relight her pipe.

Before she could even take in the face of her attacker, she found herself at the end of the alley where two cats were fighting over a fishbone. The stench of human waste and rotten meat made her gag.

"What the hell—?"

He had his hands tight around her neck and a feeling of all-encompassing power filled him with excitement. This is what he should have done to Mother. He watched Manou's face turn blue, her eyes nearly popping out of her head. He felt her last tobacco breath leave her body. As her tongue flopped from her mouth, he let her body drop to the ground.

Later, much later, Anselm felt calm as he sat with a glass of wine studying his pretty wife, whom he loathed. At any other time, listening to her incessant chatter would have made him long to hit her.

"A penny for them," she said, looking at him in the mirror.

"They ain't worth that much, and I don't think you will listen."

"Anselm, I love you. I know you never meant to hurt me."

"I can't forgive myself," said Anselm. "I love you too, and I'm just terrified of losing you."

"What do you mean?"

"I have a bad feeling. I've heard rumors."

"What rumors?"

"I don't know . . . I shouldn't say anything."

"Tell me," she said, putting her arms around him.

"Well, I have heard that Yann Margoza is a Gypsy and so is Têtu. Did you know that?"

Now he had Colombine's full attention. "That would explain that funny language they talk together."

"What I've been told is, Yann works for a man who lives in the catacombs. They are all in it together, double-dealing the clients and selling them back to the tribunal."

"No, that's not true."

"Think about it."

Colombine thought for a long time. Yann was becoming reckless. And there was that funny business with the key maker. Looking up at the cherubic face of her husband, she said, "Perhaps you're right."

"I know I am," said Anselm, with more passion than he had ever shown for her. "I think we're all in grave danger. We've got to turn Yann Margoza in, let the Commune know he's the Silver Blade. If you were to do that, we would be able to have a life together. Isn't that what you want?"

"I can't, Anselm. I can't do that, it's—"

"What?" he said, feeling his rage rise again.

What Colombine saw, or thought she saw, was Anselm trembling with passion for her, and it did her pride good.

He truly loved her.

She went up to him, and he turned and kissed her. She was taken aback by the strength of his longing. She felt shaken by that kiss. Love made her feel reckless.

Afterward, as he escorted her to the theater, he said, squeezing her hand tightly, "You've made the right decision. You won't regret it. We will do it together."

The shocking news that evening was that Citizeness Manou had been murdered. Yann was absent, on an assignment. Everyone else was cast into despair.

Pantalon said what the rest of the company was thinking. "Who would have done such a terrible thing? Isn't there enough killing in this city?"

"I think it was Yann who killed her," Anselm whispered to Colombine. "She knew too much."

Chapter Twenty-three

In Sido's dream, she hears her name being called. Walking down a woodland path she comes to a clearing. There sits an old Gypsy woman who wears many skirts of moss, of mists, of snow. In front of her is a small fire on which a kettle bubbles, its lid chattering merrily to the boiling water.

The old woman speaks with a voice that is the rustling of leaves. She calls to the spirits of the forest and, down each of the seven paths that lead into the clearing, silvery ghosts appear.

The old woman says, "Yann Margoza, Sido de Villeduval is not a Gypsy. Why is she here?"

Then she sees him standing beside the old woman, looking older than she remembers. A tiny silver thread begins spinning toward him from the shell hanging at her neck.

"Because I love her. She is the key to my soul; without her I am powerless. She has the shell, the *baro seroeske sharkuni*, the shell of the shells. Only a true Gypsy soul could benefit from its power. It will keep her safe."

The old woman turns to face Sido. In those fathomless eyes Sido sees the road unfolding and knows her journey is about to begin.

⸺

When Sido woke, her limbs ached, her eyelids fluttered against sleep and she wondered if she was back in the marquis's château, for through blurry vision she saw a canary sitting in an elaborate birdcage, singing. Slowly the chamber came into focus and, to her horror, she saw that the walls were lined with bones overlaid with gold leaf. Was she dreaming? She sat up suddenly, her head throbbing. At the end of her bed were three women servants, dressed in black.

"Where am I?"

They said nothing, but came forward and forcibly led Sido toward a bath in the middle of the room. She tried to pull free, but the women possessed an uncanny strength.

"Where am I?" she asked again.

They took no notice of anything she said, just washed and dried her, then stood her naked before a long mirror. A fine powder was blown on her until her skin had turned china-doll white. A gown of watered silk was placed over a corset and petticoats. Her hair was dressed and decorated with flowers. She saw herself disappear in the mirror.

A man came in. His face was covered in scars, like a map of a city you would never wish to visit. He had one milky eye.

"Come with me," he said.

She followed him down a corridor lined with brittle bones, still not certain if this was real or part of a kaleidoscope of dreams. She had the shell. What was the shell called? She thought if she could remember that she would be safe. It came to her: *baro seroeske sharkuni*— that was it, and walking down the haunted hall with its finger-bone lanterns blazing, she said the words over and over again, a prayer to keep her safe.

Milkeye stopped at a large, imposing door on which was written:

The dance to the hollow drum of time is done.
Here then be Death's domain.

The doors opened to reveal a long room. On one side were mirrors framed in bones. She saw chandeliers, also made of bones, candles burning, and skulls strung together and festooned across the ceiling. On the other side of the room, there were windows, blessed windows. Outside, moonlight flickered on water.

She turned away from the windows and caught her reflection in the many mirrors. She was unrecognizable, a ghost.

The doors at the other end of the room opened, and in walked Count Kalliovski, followed by seven women. He was taller than she remembered and much changed, his skin cadaverous, like waxwork rather than flesh and blood, his hair black as tar. As always, he was immaculately dressed, in a fitted black cutaway coat. He wore white lace at his neck and red kid gloves.

A living nightmare, the sight of him revolted her. His raven black, dead eyes stared straight through her. Nothing human was left in him.

He took her hand. She tried to pull away, but it was held fast in his rigor mortis grip. Raising it to his frozen lips, he kissed her palm.

"I hope you find everything to your liking." He clicked his fingers and the seven women, whose feet

261

appeared not to touch the ground, came forward. "May I introduce the Seven Sisters Macabre?"

They curtsied.

Sido stared at these horrendous apparitions and trembled. Their eyes were like glass, their skin stitched upon their faces, their mouths sewn tight shut.

When Sido had last found herself with this monster, silence had been her only power over him. Seeing the muted mouths of the Sisters Macabre, she understood that now her survival lay in words.

"I have a gift for you, one that will complement your beauty," said Count Kalliovski. He handed Sido a jewel case. She opened it and saw rubies lying there on black velvet. They made her think of blood, and she was certain this was the prelude to her death.

"Your chain first," said the count. "Allow me."

"No," said Sido, her hand reaching up to her throat, touching the shell.

The count leaned toward her, then, as if snagged on a thorn bush, he stepped back and indicated to Milkeye to remove the chain. Milkeye had no more success than his master.

Only at that moment did Sido comprehend the extraordinary nature of the talisman and, gathering her strength, she said, "This is worth more to me than all your rubies."

"It is a shell, a mere trinket. These rubies once belonged to Marie Antoinette."

"Your wealth is dust beside this shell." Every word she said made her feel a little less afraid.

Kalliovski's expression changed, or rather, since his face was incapable of such a thing, it was as if a thunderous cloud was passing overhead. His granite eyes glinted with pure malice.

"Yann Margoza gave me this talisman," she said, as if his name itself were a magic spell that might ward off evil.

"Oh? Have you wondered why Yann Margoza hasn't come to rescue you? Could it be that he no longer loves you?"

Sido bit the inside of her lip. She mustn't think about that.

"You see, he is my son. Perhaps he has taken after his father, for love corrupts, destroys, and ruins. I prefer evil. It is cleaner, has a certain honesty to it—and the devil is always so obliging."

"Your son," she said, and now she was falling, falling.

"Yes, didn't you know that? Oh dear, did he forget to mention it?"

"Yann is of Romany blood. You cannot be his father."

"But I am—and he is."

Sido instinctively clung to the shell, which suddenly glowed, warm and comforting. The light shining from it grew blindingly bright. It filled the room.

Kalliovski turned away. "Take her back to her chamber," he said to Milkeye.

To the Seven Sisters Macabre he said, "You are all dismissed."

Like a gaggle of geese, they flew at the door, eager to be gone.

Once more in her chamber, Sido sat on her bed.

What had Kalliovski said? That Yann was his *son*? It could not be. Not Yann, not her Yann.

The three harpies arrived to undress her. Exhausted, she sat in a plain linen shift, as if, having completed one dance with the devil, she was allowed to sit out the next.

In the long gallery, Kalliovski paced. How could he have been so weak as to let himself be caught off guard by a shell, a talisman? Did she know what she had around her neck? Had she any idea of the power of the *baro seroeske sharkuni*?

His gambler's instinct had been correct. Yann was in love with her. But to entrust to her such a talisman, the shell of the shells, given only to great shamans and Gypsy kings . . . He would never have been parted from it.

No, he thought bitterly, because I was not worthy of the shell of the shells. I was only worth my mother's curse. And the son I never wanted possesses what I would give my fortune for—the threads of light.

He could feel rage bubbling under the surface of his waxen skin, and another emotion, belonging to the living, so long foreign to him that it shocked him: jealousy. As he found the word, he thought he heard laughter.

He looked down the long gallery. Nobody was there.

He had convinced himself that his mind was playing tricks when Anis appeared, standing before him in all her beauty, the Madonna of the Road.

Emotions were other men's seas; he could walk on water, never plumbing the depths. Anis threatened the perfect void of his being.

She came close, her hand outstretched, and touched his waxen face.

"Dead man's skin," she said. "Do you not know that

the devil always keeps the high, wild cards for himself? You will never win at his table. Look, my murderer, at what lies at your feet."

Kalliovski stared down to see that the floor had become transparent, like an enormous dragonfly wing, and from under its iridescent surface he could see the faces of his many victims, their eyes open, staring up at him. He may have silenced the Sisters Macabre, but nothing could quiet the bodies in the grave of his conscience. He tried to move away, but Anis held him fast, forcing him to look.

A crack in the nothingness of a hollow man is a very dangerous thing, for it lets in the past and the worm of memory.

"Where is your companion?" asked Anis. "Where is Balthazar? He who never judged you, who never found you wanting? Who accepted all you did . . . except for one thing."

"What thing?"

"Forbidding him to go with the ferryman when Death came walking." She smiled. "A cruel trick, to make him live in limbo. He is another of your victims." She was in front of him, behind him, beside him, passing through him.

"Stop it, stop it!" shouted Kalliovski. The mirrors showed a multitude of his own reflections.

"Do you remember the story of the devil's dog? Tell me, how does it go, my killer?"

Giving way to a seething rage, Kalliovski picked up the jewel case and flung it at a mirror. It cracked so that he was reflected in many parts, and in none of them was he whole.

The splintered apparition of his other self spoke. "You are a dead man. I am the remains of any good that was ever in you. I am you the moment before you murdered Anis, when all roads were yours to travel, when you could have made the circle whole."

"You are nothing but a figment of my imagination!"

"I am all there is left of you," continued the apparition. "I am a small part. You belong to the grave. You are made from a dead man's bones."

Kalliovski, holding tightly to his very being, saw the apparition fade as he heard Anis sing, "We are birds, we are free."

"No, no!" he shouted.

When Milkeye returned to the chamber, he found his master bent double, his hands over his ears.

Chapter Twenty-four

Citizen Frenet and his second in command, Citizen Gabet, were on guard that night at the St. Denis gate. They were not young, and both, if they were honest, missed their beds. They'd managed to stay awake by playing cards and talking.

Citizen Frenet was a fervent sans-culotte, passionate about the Revolution and the Republic. Citizen Gabet had been a little less so since the awful business of his wife's niece, who two weeks previously had been taken to the guillotine on a trumped-up charge of conspiracy. It had frightened him, making him realize no one was safe. Frenet had little sympathy. In his eyes, the Committee of Public Safety could do no wrong.

"They would do me a great favor," he joked, "if they guillotined my wife. Now, that would be a service to the nation."

Their conversation switched to the news they had had of a colleague who had been tricked by the Silver Blade. He had had the audacity to rescue someone from the prison of La Plessis right under the guard's nose. The guard had been sent to the guillotine for his carelessness, swearing he'd been shown all the correct papers.

"Do you know what gave him away?"

"No."

"A silver blade from a child's toy guillotine. It was left hanging right above his head. I tell you," said Citizen Frenet, "if the Silver Blade were to come this way with a blank piece of paper and say it was a bona fide document, I would have him and no mistake."

"I agree," said Citizen Gabet. "I wonder if this Silver Blade ain't a bit of a myth, made up to hide slovenly practices."

"You could have a point. And all that nonsense about how it's always left hanging somewhere out of reach. I tell you, it sounds fishy."

It was then that both men nearly jumped out of their skins. Peering through the yellowed window into the smoke-filled room was a ghastly, toothless old hag.

Citizen Frenet, seeing her, grabbed hold of his pistol and went outside. The old hag was not alone; she had a friend with her who looked in an even worse way than the toothless one.

"What are you doing here? You know the penalty for being out after curfew. I'll have you arrested. Now push off!"

Gabet joined his colleague at the door.

"We should arrest them. No messing around."

The toothless one began to cough. She came closer and the smell of death on her made both guards back away.

"We've been in the Place de la Révolution," she said, spitting out her words. "Watched the scum of France lose their heads. See this blood here on my petticoat? Fresh today, it is. That's the blood of a nobleman."

"Enough," said Citizen Gabet, who knew full well what these ghastly old witches got up to, knitting at the foot of the guillotine.

"Hear that, sister? They're going to arrest us. That's kind of them, ain't it?"

Citizen Gabet noticed with alarm that her scrawny

sister seemed to be on the point of fainting. The old hag grabbed her and held her upright.

"She's been sick. That's why we weren't here earlier. Been throwing up all evening. Now she has a little rash. Go on, show these citizens that rash you've got." And the old hag made to lift her sister's skirt.

That was enough for Citizen Frenet. He knew if she had smallpox she would be infectious. Gabet, thinking the same, went to open the gate.

"Don't you want to see our documents?" said the toothless hag, and she licked her fingers and pulled the papers from her skirt.

Frenet could not bring himself to touch them, in case he too would be taken sick.

"Be gone, both of you."

"Well, I would have thought with all them stories of the Silver Blade," said the toothless hag, "you might like to—"

"Get the hell out of here. Go before I change my mind."

"As you please."

The two guards watched as, painfully slowly, they made their way into the countryside.

Back in the guardhouse, Citizen Frenet, lifting the

cognac bottle, poured some over his fingers. Citizen Gabet did the same.

"A precaution against infection," he said, and taking a mouthful from the bottle, he caught a glimmer of something silver glinting in the candlelight. The liquid ran down the side of his mouth.

"Hey, hey, don't waste it. That's good stuff."

Gabet pointed upward. The color drained from their faces.

"How the hell did that get—" Frenet rushed outside to the gate. The road was empty. He returned to the guardhouse.

"We'd better get it down. And let's agree not to tell a soul that we've been duped by the Silver Blade."

The two old hags, having rid themselves in a convenient barn of their stinking costumes, emerged as Yann Margoza and a Monsieur Bille, a terrified wig maker from Paris, who had needed almost no makeup, since fear had made the poor man look like death.

"You did well," said Yann kindly. "At least, my friend, you didn't faint."

Poor Monsieur Bille was speechless. All he could do was nod. Only when Yann handed him over to a trusted bargeman at Port du Gravier did the wig maker recover.

Yann returned to Paris later that night, sure he was being followed. Once again he sensed Balthazar close on his heels. When he caught sight of him in the moonlight, through some beech trees, he was monstrously large.

What is it he wants from me? Yann asked himself. The great beast slowly raised his head and stared straight at him. Yann's blood ran cold. Once he had spoken to the soul of the hound, but Balthazar no longer had the eyes of a dog. Those brown orbs of love and devotion had been replaced by human eyes. Yann had no words that could touch him. Then the beast was gone.

With a jolt Yann remembered the story of the devil's dog, and knew that the spirit of *beng,* the evil one, was out walking. He trembled for himself; he trembled for Paris.

He was relieved to be back in the city once more. Still trying to shake off the image of those human eyes, it came to him that it wasn't Balthazar who was evil, but his master. Kalliovski was responsible for the dog's plight. Yann felt overcome by pity for the dog and for all those caught up in this bloodbath. Pity for those never to be remembered: the curtain maker, pleased to dress the tall windows of Versailles; the hosier, whose silk stockings the king wore to his death; the tax collector, who brought in the revenue; the banker who sent money abroad to an émigré client. Pity the seamstress who sewed the queen's hems; the butcher who hoarded; the wife who whispered a confession to a priest. Pity France. What a sorrowful city Paris had become. And spare some pity for yourself, Yann. Perhaps Têtu was right. It would have been better if I had never known about Kalliovski, for the knowledge is a cancer that has eaten its way into my soul.

That night, as with many nights when he wasn't on stage, he felt lost. He had put away all Sido's letters and would not allow himself to look at them. He had thought of burning them, but the idea of never seeing even her words again made him unbearably sad. As usual, he sought comfort at the café on the square.

Têtu had witnessed Yann's descent into deep melancholy and was powerless to help. Everything he suggested, Yann rejected. He disregarded Têtu's carefully laid plans for escapes, choosing instead to go about things in his own idiosyncratic way. If a priest knew where to find the Silver Blade, it would not be long before the authorities managed to work it out. It was as if Yann wanted to be caught. Even faithful Didier, who would have followed him to hell and back, was bewildered by the change in him. The only person who benefitted was Anselm. For if Yann had been his old self, Anselm would never again have had access to the theater, but somehow he had taken over Citizeness Manou's job, and Yann made no protest.

Têtu had waited anxiously for Yann at the theater. He needed time alone with him; there was news that he didn't want to tell him publicly. But Yann had avoided him, as he often did these days. Têtu found him seated with Pantalon at the middle table, engrossed in a card game. Anselm was watching with Colombine, whose arms were wrapped around his neck. She was wearing a small pair of guillotine earrings, which were all the fashion in Paris.

Têtu pushed his way to the table. "I need to speak to you, Yannick."

"Not now. I'm on a winning streak. Look what I inherited from my father. Good at cards. The jack of diamonds, that's me."

"Yann, please, now. It's urgent."

"No, Têtu, leave me alone."

"Why don't you talk French, you two," said Colombine, "instead of that gibberish none of us can understand. What language is it you're speaking anyway?"

Têtu ignored her. His presence began to irritate Yann.

"Go away, Têtu. It can wait till the morning. There, I win."

"This afternoon I saw Cordell. Serious news has arrived posthaste from London—"

"Damn it," said Pantalon. "Another hand?"

What Têtu had to say couldn't wait.

"Last week Sido was abducted. There was no note, no trace left behind."

Yann found that he had lost his appetite for cards and wine. Sobriety hit him abruptly in the face.

"Who . . ." He swallowed. ". . . How did it happen?"

"She was leaving Mr. Trippen's. He was shot trying to save her."

"Is he . . . dead?"

"No. The doctors believe he will recover. The Laxtons expected a ransom note, but then they had word that she had been found."

"Thank God," said Yann. "Is she all right?"

"Her body was recovered from one of the ponds on Hampstead Heath. It had been in the water, they think, for a week."

Yann could no longer hear any voices, only the drum of blood beating in his ears. Had everything stopped? He couldn't tell. He couldn't breathe.

Têtu saw the brightly colored threads that danced around Yann fade before his eyes. The young man staggered to his feet, his face bloodless.

"What is it?" said Colombine, looking frightened. "*Chéri*, speak to me! What's wrong with you?"

He pushed past Colombine, knocking over the card table.

"Hey," shouted Pantalon, "that was a winning hand." Yann, gasping for air like a drowning man, made it out to the street before he spewed up half his insides.

Chapter Twenty-five

Têtu was talking to him, and yet he heard nothing. He felt Têtu put something in his jacket pocket . . . but he was falling, falling, and had a long way to go. Sick to his soul, he stumbled into the night, so lost he hardly knew where he was going. Sido's death stripped Yann of his powers; the threads of light had gone, disappeared from his vision. He was blind.

He went down to the Seine and sat on an upturned boat. Tonight they could arrest him, he didn't care. They could guillotine him, he didn't care. He would willingly lay his head on the block, as if it were a feather pillow. How could he go on living if there was no Sido? Without her, time had stopped. She would always remain in yesterday. He felt Paris wrap itself around him, a city of the broken embracing a broken man.

I want Sido to be alive. I want to hold her. To love her, to tell her the truth. I want to have lain with her, to have been beloved of her, always. And in that I would have known I was blessed upon this earth. The luckiest of men.

At dawn, Paris was almost quiet, as if she was holding her breath, the city trembling at what the new day might bring. In its watery light, Yann found something in his pocket. It was an envelope.

He opened it, pulled out a letter and straightened it. The words danced away from him until he made them stay still long enough to read.

I have something that I wish to tell you. I couldn't live like this all my life, a doll in a dolls' house. I long for adventure, I long to be free, I want to ride with you across moors, through forests. I want to travel with you across the seas. I don't want a painted ceiling in a bedroom. I want the stars, I want to lie with you on the mossy grass in fields of poppies, in haylofts of gold, to be with you always.

I am not a marquis's daughter, Yann. I was born the wrong side of an unhappy marriage. What use is a title? I give it away.

There. Anyone can have this iron cage full of prejudice
and privilege. I want to be plain Madame Margoza. That
has a freedom to it, that has wind in its sails.

Never, ever, Yann, tell me that your being a Gypsy
would stop me loving you. I too have a Gypsy soul. I am
yours and only yours.

Sido

Yann felt as if he had been mortally wounded by his
own hand, his own folly. This was the letter he'd given
back to Têtu, unread. He thought of what Sido had
received from him in return, his short letter cutting her
off from him.

And now it was too late.

"I must go to London," he said out loud, as if emerging from a fog. His words sounded awkward, his tongue
heavy as lead. He never wanted to talk to anyone ever
again if he couldn't talk to Sido. And by the waters of
the Seine he wept.

Didier had been out since dawn looking for him. Now,
having as good as scoured Paris, he decided to go back
to the Circus of Follies.

The barman at the café on the corner was sweeping

out the sawdust, the tables and chairs stacked in the morning sunlight.

"Citizen," he called to Didier, "have you found him?"

Didier shook his head. The barman brought him coffee.

Didier drank it and was about to leave when the barman said, "It looks as if Citizen Aulard has the inspectors in again."

Didier, thinking nothing of it, entered the theater by the stage door. He'd started up the stairs to Citizen Aulard's office when, too late, he saw five National Guardsmen on the landing, their pistols cocked. He turned to run when two more armed guards stood up in the concierge's sentry box, their weapons aimed straight at him. Didier was chained and taken onto the stage. The rest of the company, including Anselm, was there, surrounded by soldiers.

"Is that everyone?" said the sergeant, catching Anselm's eye. The look that passed between them didn't escape Didier's notice.

Didier, a giant of a man and stronger by the power of ten when angry, rushed at Anselm and with one punch hit him halfway across the stage. The guards descended on him like wasps on jam, but even in chains, Didier knocked three of them unconscious before the sergeant restored order by firing his pistol at the ceiling.

"You've broken my nose," whined Anselm. Then seeing everyone's sharp eyes on him, including Colombine's, he said, "Don't look at me. She's in on it too."

"Quiet, not another word," said the sergeant.

While Anselm and Colombine were taken away separately, the sergeant said, "You are all under arrest. All of you are suspects. Things might go better if you tell us which of your company goes by the name of the Silver Blade."

Silence.

"I ask you again, and this will be the last time. Which of you is the Silver Blade?"

And again no one said a word.

"To the Conciergerie with the lot of you."

The barman at the corner café on the square stared openmouthed in horror to see nearly all his regular customers from the Circus of Follies chained together and loaded onto the waiting wagons like sheep.

"Oh, these are the days of murder and mourning," he muttered miserably to himself.

The only two persons missing from this sorry band were Têtu and Basco.

"Where are they?" asked Didier.

"Têtu went to see Cordell," whispered Citizen Aulard. "Basco accompanied him." Iago was perched on his shoulder.

"Good."

"Cordell wanted to see you too. Oh, God, what's going to happen to us?"

"I would have thought," said Didier, avoiding the subject, "that you'd have left the parrot behind."

"So would I, but Iago was adamant."

Didier looked at the cart carrying Anselm and Colombine. What we do for love, he thought. Still, he would have imagined Colombine to have had more sense than to fall for that thug. He turned his back on them and instead watched the city he loved roll slowly past, saying a long farewell to his freedom. By the time the turrets of the Conciergerie came into view, the sky had turned ominously black, the air laden with the approaching storm.

In the past, when there was still justice in France, this palace had been its seat. But justice had long been banished, and the palace was home to the dreaded

Revolutionary Tribunal and its tyrannical ruler, the hatchet-man of the convention, Fouquier-Tinville. It contained within its weather-stained stone walls one of the most notorious prisons in Paris. The sight of those infamous gates sent a ripple of fear through the whole company. This was where Marie Antoinette had been imprisoned; through these gates Danton had been taken in a tumbrel on his way to execution. The list was growing, day by day, of the great and the good who had been sacrificed to the pernicious new ruler of France—the guillotine.

It was not surprising, then, that the company was trembling as they stepped from the wagons. Pantalon was a sorry sight, makeup running, knees knocking, as he and the rest were unceremoniously prodded and pushed, unable to hear themselves think above the barking of the dogs. They were ushered through more gates and doors, which clanged shut and locked behind them, then down a long stone corridor. There they were left waiting on a bench in a sunless place whose walls seemed to sweat tears.

Opposite was a small room, and through the filthy glass, they could see the prison governor seated in his armchair in front of a wooden table. Above and below, a tangle of sounds reverberated: the turn of a key, the echo of footsteps, the cries of a prisoner, laughter and the clang of a bell. All were separated by impenetrable silence, and still they waited. Tick . . . tock. Tick . . . tock.

Time imprisoned here was thin and whispery, its beat almost lost in the dungeons.

The prison governor seemed not to have noticed the new arrivals, or that one of them had a parrot on his head, for never once did he bother to look in their direction. Only a rat appeared interested in them, sniffing the air before scurrying under the bench. Colombine let out a gasp.

"Quiet," boomed the guard. His dog looked hungry and mean, ready to tear to pieces anyone who crossed him.

"You there," said a turnkey, breaking the silence, pointing at Anselm. "The governor is waiting."

A few minutes later Anselm came out, and avoiding all eye contact, walked to the end of the corridor, where a door, unlit and unseen by those left seated, opened.

Then he was gone.

Colombine was next to be summoned, followed by Pantalon, and after a short interview each was taken out through the door at the end of the corridor. This routine went on until only Citizen Aulard and Didier were left.

"Do you think they betrayed us?" asked Citizen Aulard gloomily.

***

What had saved Yann from returning to the theater that fateful morning was exhaustion. It had finally overcome him, and he had curled up and slept under a tarpaulin in the bottom of a broken boat. He had woken with a start around midday and for a moment, one blissful moment, all looked right with the world. Then he remembered.

Slowly he made his way back to the Place de Manon.

"At least," said the barman, his hand on Yann's sleeve, "you have been spared. I feel terrible."

Yann looked at him, bewildered.

"I mean, I didn't know," continued the barman, making no sense whatsoever.

"Know what?" asked Yann.

The barman pulled him inside the café.

"I didn't know the National Guard was in there waiting to arrest everyone. Early this morning they took all the members of the Circus of Follies away in tumbrels to the Conciergerie."

What have I done? thought Yann. I have let so many people down.

"I heard," said the barman, "that they think they've caught the Silver Blade."

Chapter Twenty-six

Sido was wearing a heavily embroidered gown. Her hair was dressed high on her head and sprinkled with diamonds. Though the shell was still resting safely at her neck, in the mirror she saw someone else, someone completely detached from herself.

Milkeye escorted her into the dining chamber, where the candles were all alight and the long table laid as if for many guests, decorated with bowls of sugared fruit and silver vases of lilies. The blooms were fleshlike, their smell heady.

Sido was wondering who would be joining them when she noticed, in the center of the table, a strange cake stand. What delicacy was hidden behind the frosted glass, she couldn't imagine.

Kalliovski not so much entered the room as materialized, seated at the end of the table. With him was Balthazar. Sido was taken aback at the size of the dog. He was more like a huge wolf of almost mythical proportions. And his terrifying eyes were all too human. He snarled, revealing a mouthful of pointed teeth, and Sido noticed that Kalliovski held the dog tightly on a chain.

They sat together in silence, Kalliovski studying her closely until Sido, unable to stand his gaze any longer, asked, "You are expecting other guests?"

"All my many friends," he replied.

Still no one came. He clicked his fingers and Milkeye poured champagne for her, and her alone, and served her tasteless morsels of food. Kalliovski watched. He neither drank nor ate, but then, addressing Milkeye, he said, "The Marquis de Villeduval might like to join us."

Sido stopped eating and watched in horror as the frosted glass of the cake stand was pulled back to reveal the marquis's lifelike head. She stood up, knocking over her champagne. The delicate, fluted glass shattered on the stone floor.

She ran to the door. Milkeye barred her exit.

"You always were so clumsy, Sidonie," said the head

of the marquis, "and I see that there is little improvement."

Sido closed her eyes and put her hands over her ears. She willed the room to disappear. Milkeye held the chair for her to be reseated.

The marquis said, "And you still have that irritating limp, Sidonie."

Sido had lost her voice. She was shaking.

The head sniffed in the exact same way the marquis used to. Everything about him seemed so real. This was the devil's work.

On Kalliovski's orders, Milkeye lifted up the contraption and moved it closer to her.

"I knew things were coming to a pretty pass when ladies stopped wearing corsets," said the severed head of the marquis.

"He is, you must agree," said Kalliovski, "a lot more entertaining—and much less expensive—now he is dead."

"Stop it!" shouted Sido. "Stop this charade. What do you want of me? You have done enough. You have ruined our family, had the marquis killed—what more do you want?"

"That is a little exaggerated. I once wanted you for

my bride, and if you had done as you were bid, I would be a different man. No, instead you ran away. I told you I never forget."

"He has no mercy. He shows no mercy," said the marquis's head.

Sido rose to her feet and, regardless of Milkeye, refused to sit down again. "I will not stay here. I would rather go to the guillotine than stay here."

"There is no need to overexcite yourself. Such drama. I always remembered you as so silent, so interesting. Give me the shell and you shall have your freedom." Kalliovski spoke with calculated precision.

"May your soul burn in hell!"

"The marquis always was very wrong about you, wasn't he?" said Kalliovski. "A foolish man. If you've had enough to eat, let me show you something."

He came closer and the temperature in the room grew colder. Sido shivered. The red glove stroked her face and she flinched. He took her hand and led her to a room adjoining the dining chamber.

"Here are my guests."

On several benches stood rows of heads. On the shelves above were glass jars containing organs. Artificial limbs hung from the ceiling.

"This," said Kalliovski, "is where I make my automata. I have a choice of heads from the guillotine, for I don't forget my friends. I have death masks taken of those I knew so that they may keep me company. This one is Remon Quint, the renowned key maker."

"Why are you showing me these obscenities?"

"Because if you don't give me the shell, I will be forced to take more drastic measures, and if those measures result in your death, so be it. As an automaton you will be more beautiful, I think, than the Sisters Macabre, and you will keep me company for all eternity. I might make you my bride after all."

Sido backed away as Kalliovski addressed the head of the key maker. "Such a pity you couldn't dine with us tonight," he said.

Remon Quint's eyes opened.

"Citizen Quint, may I introduce you to the Marquise Sidonie de Villeduval. Tell her what you've made for me."

"A key."

"Tell her what kind of key."

"A key to a soul."

"Such a key is impossible," said Sido.

Kalliovski's laughter, like the drone of bees, traveled

around the chamber, his words stinging her. "Nothing is impossible. Citizen Quint, tell her whose soul it is the key to."

"Yann Margoza's," said the key maker.

Kalliovski clicked his fingers and the heavy eyelids of Remon Quint closed abruptly.

Sido shuddered. "The shell would never belong to such a one as you."

"Consider my offer, for I will not make it again. Take her back to her chamber."

Mr. Tull, accompanied by Anselm, waited in the long gallery for his master. Anselm was tapping his foot, looking more restless and disturbed than Tull had ever seen him.

Mr. Tull was feeling nervous too. For all his assiduous planning, the kidnapping of Sido de Villeduval hadn't turned out well. No, indeed it hadn't.

"He wasn't my father, was he?" said Anselm, turning on Mr. Tull.

"Who wasn't?"

"The butcher Loup. He wasn't."

"Don't ask me, I don't know. He said he was."

"He was a liar, he only said that to protect the master."

"What are you on about? You've been down here a bit too long. Sent your brain mushy, has it?"

"You see, I know. I know the very truth of truths."

"Good for you," said Mr. Tull, thinking once again that the boy seemed more than a bit odd.

"It's Count Kalliovski."

"What is?" said Mr. Tull. "You've lost me there."

Anselm's foot was now tapping a frenzied beat. "No, I mean, I am Kalliovski's son."

"Look, could you stop fidgeting? You've been drinking, haven't you?"

"No. I just know I'm the devil's son."

"Well, that ain't a lie," said Mr. Tull. "He has a few, so I'm told."

"No, you see, you don't understand. I am the master's one and only son," said Anselm, grabbing Mr. Tull by his coat.

"Get off me! What the hell is wrong with you? You're talking absolute gibberish. Bloody Frenchman!"

They both turned and jumped to see Kalliovski sitting in a wing-back chair, listening to them.

"Anselm," he said, "wait outside."

Anselm, suddenly calm, did as he was told without a word.

"You have let me down," said Kalliovski as the door closed.

"No, master, it wasn't my fault. I did everything to the letter, but I wasn't to know they would find a body in the Hampstead pond, and that some buffoon would think it was Sido de Villeduval."

Kalliovski sat looking at him. "Then you had better find another way to bring Yann Margoza to me."

"I have, I've got a plan. Anselm has already put it into action."

"This does not reassure me," said Kalliovski as he slowly peeled off one of his red kid gloves.

Mesmerized, Mr. Tull could not look away. He felt an insane urge to burst out laughing when he saw that the hand was just like any other man's. Slowly Kalliovski took off the second red, bright red, poppy red glove to reveal his other hand. A skeleton hand. He beckoned Mr. Tull, spinning sticky threads of darkness from his fingers. Mr. Tull moved closer, and his screams choked in his throat as the skeleton hand almost throttled him to death.

"Do not fail me if you ever wish to grow cabbages in Kent."

"I won't. I've got a plan," gasped Mr. Tull.

Next to see his master was Anselm.

"So, you think you are my son?" said Kalliovski. "What makes you believe you could ever belong to me?"

Anselm felt his words, knife-sharp, cutting through his reason. "I was left in—"

"A basket of stinking animal entrails. But that doesn't make you my son. No, you see, you are a common murderer. Take the killing of Citizeness Manou. You kill like a coward, full of rage. Rage will be your undoing. I have never murdered anyone in anger." As he said it, he thought he heard Anis laughing. "Anger is an emotion that is useless unless properly controlled. It will destroy you."

"I know I am—"

"Know? You don't know anything. You understand even less," said Kalliovski. "If you can bring me the shell from Sido de Villeduval's neck, then perhaps I will find some use for you. If you fail me in this . . ." Kalliovski was now beside him, his breath coffin-stale. "If you fail me, however hard you try to disappear, know this: I will find you. Were I you, I wouldn't trust my own shadow."

Chapter Twenty-seven

Sido found herself once more dressed in a plain linen gown. This time the dance had nearly defeated her. Curled on the bed, her knees pulled up tightly toward her chest, she felt her courage ebb. The shadows were closing in, and she knew she was completely alone. How long would this torture go on before Kalliovski decided to murder her?

She closed her eyes against the inevitable and, for a moment she wasn't sure if she was asleep or awake, for when she opened them, a woman was sitting beside her. Her clothes were colorful and bright; she was dressed as for some strange fete. Her hair was jet black, she had dark eyes, high cheekbones, and a full mouth, and in that face Sido saw someone she recognized.

"I am Anis," said the woman, "mother of Yann. Come, I have something to show you."

She held Sido's hand as the walls of bone faded and were replaced by a deep mist. When it cleared, they were walking over the rooftops of Paris and then down into a dark courtyard where the tumbrels waited to take the condemned to die.

Sido turned to look at Anis. "What are we doing here?" she asked. "This is the Conciergerie."

Anis put her finger to her lips as like two ghosts they drifted down the cold corridors. The smells and noises of the prison brought back memories of the Abbaye and filled Sido with dread. Now they were in a tiny cell and there, lying on a narrow bed, was a young man.

"No," said Sido. "No! What is Yann doing here? Tell me this is not so, tell me this hasn't happened."

"This is now, and his end will be tomorrow, but for you."

"I don't understand. You talk in riddles."

"Go to him."

Sido sat beside him. He looked through her and said to the air, "Sido."

"I am here."

"He can't hear you," said Anis, "and he can't see you.

He is broken by the knowledge of who he believes his father to be. I would never have had him learn of it. It is this knowledge that makes him think you will love him no more."

"That is not so. Why can't I tell him? Yann . . ."

"Come."

"No, wait. I must tell him . . ."

She felt Anis's hand in hers and once more they were traveling, this time out of the city over treetops to where, in a woodland clearing, a young man stood laughing among a group of Gypsies. Sido wondered if this too was Yann, for he looked so like him.

"This is Manouche," said Anis. "This is the man I love. He is Yann's spirit father."

Then Sido saw soldiers coming through the trees, saw bright flashes from their muskets.

"Warn them!" Sido shouted. "Why don't they run? We must help them!"

"This is the past. What has been done is done. No tomorrows can unpick history."

The guns fired again. The acrid smoke cleared and all was quiet, all were dead.

Once more Anis took Sido's hand and they rose higher to see scorched earth in the clearing below them.

In the burned trees hung the bodies of the Gypsies, like broken birds of paradise.

In the room of bone once more, Sido longed to hold fast to Anis so that she might never leave her. She felt Anis's fingers, velvet-soft, touch her face as she whispered, as if in prayer:

"That is the shell of the shells he gave thee.
You are blessed, he loves thee much.
Don't be afraid, stand up.
He is within you as I am beside you,
You are one with us.
Yann is Manouche's ghost child. Don't lose faith."

Anis kissed her in the middle of her forehead and was gone.

The sleep that followed was deep and peaceful. Sido woke to find an angel in her room, his golden hair, his amber eyes so luminous that she wondered if she was still dreaming. She sat up knowing, as if Anis were whispering to her, that this was no angel. This was death's seducer.

Anselm, for once, was at a loss, for never before had he seen a creature more beautiful than himself.

"My master wants to know if you will give him the shell." His voice was almost a whisper.

"No," said Sido.

"My master says he will have it from you whether you are dead or alive."

The memory of Anis's words gave her courage. "Leave me be and tell your master my answer is still no."

Anselm couldn't understand why he felt no anger. Usually by now such obstinacy would have been enough to rouse the red dragon in him, but looking into Sido's blue eyes he felt almost at peace, the flame beneath the cauldron of his fury spent.

He tried again, hoping to ignite something in himself that would make it possible to take hold of her and pull the shell from her neck. He went closer. It would be so easy, and then Kalliovski would embrace him as his son.

Sido stood up. For a moment he wasn't quite sure what had happened, for she began to fade away in front of his eyes. All he could see was a blinding light coming from the shell. It felt like the sun burning him. Try as he might, he could get no closer. The light was so strong. He knew he was defeated and, turning, he ran like the devil's own wind from the room. Outside, Milkeye watched him go and knew he wouldn't be returning.

Kalliovski, looking out of his window at his artificial garden, was told of Anselm's failure.

"A pity. Sido leaves me no alternative," he said.

Behind him stood the Seven Sisters and, from one glass eye of each, a tear rolled without permission down their dead-skin faces.

"So," said Kalliovski, "there will be another to keep us company."

He rose and, hauling on Balthazar's heavy chain, said to him, "You may have the first and the last taste of her innocent beauty, that is my gift to you."

At Sido's chamber, Kalliovski removed his poppy red glove. From his skeleton fingertips, skeins of black threads hungrily searched out the lock in the iron door.

At a signal from his master, Milkeye opened the leather case containing Remon Quint's key. The dark threads seemed to devour it as they pushed it into the lock.

The door opened. Kalliovski freed Balthazar from his spiked collar and let the ravenous hound in, swiftly closing the door behind him. Sido's scream filled the air. As he walked away, his red-heeled boots clicking on the stone, he heard the howl of a hungry dog.

Chapter Twenty-eight

"What is your name?" The prison governor looked down the list.

"Yann Margoza."

He had been caught as he was leaving the café. He had no will to fight. In a strange way he was relieved that at last it was over. Death finally had ahold of him.

"Well, now, isn't that interesting? And they tell me you're the Silver Blade. Are you?"

"There is no such person," said Yann. "It's a myth."

"I agree. I wouldn't have believed it unless I'd been told," said the governor, leaning back in the armchair. "I always imagined the Silver Blade to be older, and to be an Englishman."

Yann stayed silent. He didn't feel that anything he had to say would make the situation any better.

The prisoner governor laughed. "There I was, fishing for trout, when I went and caught myself the biggest pike in the river."

He turned to the theater manager. "You have never heard of the Silver Blade either?"

Citizen Aulard shook his head, hoping to goodness Iago would keep quiet. Lord knows what Têtu had taught him to say.

"I would make the most of all that head-shaking while you still have one," the governor said, pen in hand.

Yann concentrated hard on him; the pain was like burning rods pushing through his eyes. He knew his powers were nearly too weak to catch the governor's mind, full as it was with confused indictments.

The governor signed the paper before him and called for a turnkey. "This one is to be taken to the Luxembourg prison."

Citizen Aulard was completely baffled by what had just happened. The Luxembourg meant a chance of survival, whereas to remain at the Conciergerie was certain death. He was about to say something when the parrot squawked, *"Vive la Nation!"*

"That's a very talented bird you have there," said the prison governor, indicating to the turnkey to take Citizen Aulard away.

He returned to the matter at hand. "As for you, Citizen Margoza, and you, Citizen Didier, you two are under arrest on the serious charge of being counterrevolutionaries and working against this great and glorious Republic. Both of you will be sent for trial." He nodded to the guard. "Take them away."

They walked along the dimly lit corridor, passing rows of cells where the cries of anguished men rose and fell. In the last glimpse that Yann had of the outside world, the skies opened and rain splashed upon the cobbles, puffs of dust rising with the water. Citizen Aulard was standing in a wagon, soaking wet, looking more like a martyred saint than ever. Iago, on the other hand, his head held high, looked like a hero of the cause.

Yann was separated from Didier and escorted by three guards into a small cubicle, the floor of which was covered in hair. The barber, obviously drunk, stood swaying, a filthy leather apron tied around his waist. Yann struggled as he was pushed down in the chair, knowing what was to come.

"Cut it off," said his guard.

"Will all the ladies be weeping?" the barber inquired as he went to work.

Still Yann said nothing as the scissors cut irregular chunks off his hair. Chop, chop, chop. A foretaste of the blade to come.

"Makes it easier," said the barber. He took a swig of wine from the bottle next to his instruments on the table. "As I was saying, it makes it easier for the blade of the guillotine to cut through the flesh and bone." Yann was locked in a small cell containing a bed and a pail, which smelled as if it hadn't been emptied since the last occupant left.

Thunder started to rumble, and lightning illuminated his cell. Lying on the hard wooden bed, he thought, Tonight is my last night on earth. Tomorrow my life will be over and I care little.

Yet he felt uneasy, not about his own death, no . . . And in one flash of lightning it came to him. What if the body found in a Hampstead pond wasn't Sido's? Where was she?

He sat upright. It was as if Sido were with him, beside him, giving him the answer. He was a fool not to have thought of it before, a dunce, a numskull! And now he was caught, locked away in one of the most notorious prisons in France.

If she was alive, the only man who would have taken her was Count Kalliovski.

At about three in the morning, the grille in the iron door to Yann's cell slid open. He heard a guard ask, "Is this the one?" Then, "How do you want to do it?"

The door opened and Yann tried to see the threads of light. If he could make them work again, he could escape. He looked from one prison guard to the other, but could only read their thoughts—a jumble that gave him no clues. Two more burst into the cell, pinning him down while his mouth was wrenched open and foul-tasting liquid was poured down his throat. Yann's eyes felt heavy and almost immediately his limbs seemed to fill with lead. His vision dissolved like ink in water, and he heard a crash, a curse, and smelled what must have been the spilled contents of the pail. The stench, as good as smelling salts, revived him, before more liquid was forced down his throat. He gagged. Lightning lit up the cell, and Milkeye's face loomed monster-large over him. Then all went black.

Yann woke. His mouth was dry, his head hurt, his face was cut and bruised. He was lying on a damp stone floor in a vaulted chamber, the walls lined with human bones. It took a moment for the room to stop spinning, for him to find his feet.

Now he was wide-awake and, like a cat sensing danger, he took in his surroundings, looking for a way out. At one end of the chamber there was a door, while at the other side were two smaller doors under a wooden gantry. He could smell a familiar mustiness, which no amount of incense could hide. He knew he was under the city. Suddenly the chamber became ice cold.

He turned to face his fear and understood then that there is no greater devil than the fiend we invent for ourselves.

Had he really lost his powers because of this living waxwork? Let a man that was neither of the grave nor of life ruin his future? He thought back to when he had seen Kalliovski on the Pont Neuf before the mob claimed him. At least then he was made of flesh and blood. Now he bore merely a passing resemblance to the man he had once been. He was still immaculately dressed, his face waxen smooth, his hair powdered, and his eyes shining with an insect intensity. But they were the eyes of a dead man.

Yann watched Kalliovski pull off one of his red kid gloves to reveal a skeleton hand. From his waistcoat pocket he took out a long silver chain, at the end of which was a key. Idly he began to swing it back and forth.

"This is the key I commissioned Remon Quint to make. Do you know what it is the key to?"

"No," said Yann.

"It is the key to your soul."

Yann's laughter sounded like fresh water in a desert. "You're mad if you think such a thing is possible. Quite mad, deluded by your own desire."

"No," said Kalliovski quietly. "I am in earnest. If you show me the secret of the threads of light, I will give you back your soul."

"I don't need your key to own my soul."

"Don't you understand? I have Sido de Villeduval. I will give her her freedom, let you take her out of the catacombs, if you give me the secret of the threads of light."

Yann felt a surge of strength. At last he was close to her. He would not fail. His words now were measured. "You, more than I, should know it is not mine to give away. It is within me, as is my heart and soul. The devil duped you. You are the one in chains."

Kalliovski pointed his skeleton finger at Yann. For a moment Yann could not think what he was doing; then he saw dark sticky threads snake their way toward him. They wrapped themselves around his waist, lifting him toward the vaulted bare-boned ceiling.

Kalliovski released the dark threads and Yann tumbled like a falling star onto the unforgiving floor.

"So, you have lost your powers," said the count. "I should have known as much. What a pity. I was looking forward to a duel. My powers will never leave me. Unlike yours, they don't toss and turn on a sea of emotions. And there I was thinking that they might be something to master. You are not worthy to be my son."

Yann became aware of a figure in the chamber, the woman he had seen in the field, all golden. He heard her laughing and knew Kalliovski heard her too.

"You are not my father," said Yann, knowing that he was at last speaking the truth and feeling freedom in that knowledge. "I am a ghost-child. Listen, my mother is still laughing. Take me to Sido."

"Certainly, but she is dead. You see, I asked her courteously for the talisman, but she has a willful streak. Or perhaps it was for love of you that she refused to relinquish it. I offered her Marie Antoinette's ruby necklace in exchange and still . . . There was no alternative. I had to put Balthazar in with her, and he has an insatiable appetite for human flesh. No doubt he is licking her bones clean as we speak."

"I don't believe you," said Yann, knowing that if he showed any emotion, all would be lost.

"It doesn't matter whether you believe me or not. If she's dead I will make her whole again. I have that power. She will be my finest automaton yet." Kalliovski clapped his hands. "You shall see for yourself."

Milkeye appeared and led Yann along a corridor lined with skeleton hands holding dripping candles.

At the door to Sido's chamber, the dog's barking, wild and furious, was deafening. Once more Kalliovski sent out the dark threads, turning the key slowly in the lock.

Yann, his heart beating fast, felt he was standing on the very edge of his existence. If she was dead, he knew he had no soul to fight for.

He didn't flinch as the door creaked open. At first, all he could see was Balthazar, his troubled eyes all too human. The rest of the room was hidden by his bulk. Yann could hear his thoughts: I have waited. Where have you been? I called for you and you didn't come, I followed you and you didn't see me.

It wasn't Yann who backed away, it was the master and his servant. Count Kalliovski, with a rattle and a clang, slammed the door shut. Yann was in the room with Balthazar.

And then there was silence except for Balthazar's panting. He stayed where he was until, hearing his master's red heels retreat down the corridor, he moved farther into the chamber toward a bed, where he lay down at Sido's feet.

She stood there, the tamer of wolves, in a white linen shift, her dark hair curled around her shoulders, her blue eyes shining like a cloudless day. Yann was filled with a wondrous relief. She was alive, unharmed. From the shell at her neck threads of light danced, spinning toward him, reeling him in. She shimmered as her hand touched his and, as he wrapped her in his arms, he felt the softness of her skin and the warmth of her body, made of the flesh and blood of mortality. He found her sweet mouth; her kiss sent a jolt right through him. The threads of light had returned to their master.

He whispered, "Sido, if we get out of this, will you forgive . . . ?"

She kissed him. "Balthazar and I have been waiting for you. He has been waiting a long, long time."

Yann looked into the face of the great beast and began to talk to him as once, long ago, he had talked to him in the library at the Marquis de Villeduval's château. And the great dog listened. The great dog spoke. Yann understood.

Standing, he held Sido once more to him. She smelled of the future, a perfume filled with the promise of life and days to come.

Chapter Twenty-nine

It was the dog's size that undid Kalliovski. He could ignore Balthazar's human eyes, but this . . . this tore at the worn fabric of his sanity. Memories, butchered and disjointed, came back to him: of a caravan, a baby crying, of Balthazar, his brown eyes devoted, of Anis telling him of the two roads she'd seen on his palm. He knew all too well the danger of letting light into rooms where no light has been. It illuminated images from a life he would rather not revisit. A grief was engulfing him, finding the cracks and fissures, tearing at the seams of his existence.

What was happening to him? A story, fragments of an old Gypsy tale, jostled in his head: *The day the devil went walking, looking for one irredeemable soul to blow his fiery life into.* How did it go? He should remember. "And he called to the devil's dog and the devil's dog said, 'Master, I am here to take you . . .'"

"Stop it, stop it! Silence! Why isn't there silence?"

Milkeye looked at his master. He'd never seen him like this before. Kalliovski pulled off his red glove and stared at his skeleton hand as if expecting it to turn to dust.

"If I had the threads of light I would be whole again, complete. I must have the threads of light."

Balthazar's howl, low and long, rumbled like thunder through the echo-less chambers. A warning from the mouth of hell.

"He's coming for me. He's coming for me. I must stop him."

There was a deafening sound as if a battering ram was knocking down the door. Kalliovski did his best to concentrate on the dark threads and nothing else, but still there was the endless noise in his head, like the chattering teeth of the key maker before he was killed.

Then all was eerily quiet, and Kalliovski knew Yann's threads of light had defeated the key maker's masterpiece.

He heard the iron claws approach and Balthazar,

magnificent, majestic, walked in, head held high, Sido and Yann in his wake.

Kalliovski stood straight, determined that this must be his victory. He had planned it all and this hour had been purchased by him. As Balthazar stared, his master, unblinking, threw out the dark threads. The threads snaked toward Balthazar and, plaiting themselves together, formed a hangman's knot around his neck. The great dog's gaze never left his master.

Kalliovski's laughter filled the chamber and he pulled with all his might, tighter and tighter, forcing open the monstrous mouth. No more would men be killed by those jaws. Still the dog stared with knowing eyes while the dark threads cut into his coal black fur. Then his huge paws slid, and he lay on the ground, his countenance ghastly, his tongue lolling, his blank eyes accusing the master who had slain him. Inky liquid oozed from between his steely teeth. The enormous beast was no more.

"You thought you could outwit me," said Kalliovski, his reason teetering on the brink of madness. "I will be all powerful. I will have the light and the dark. I will have my revenge. Take off the talisman."

As Yann took the shell from Sido's neck, he was illuminated, made radiant by the power of the *baro seroeske sharkuni*. He held it out to Kalliovski.

"No!" Kalliovski bellowed, nearly blinded as the light grew stronger, encompassing Sido. "Stand away from her or I will kill her, like I killed . . ." He stopped, pierced by the sharp bee sting of a memory. How did the story go? *The devil's dog* . . . What was it Anis had told him when she had seen his future, all those years ago? *Two roads, one light, one dark* . . .

"Like you killed my mother? You will not take Sido from me."

"You cannot stop me," said Kalliovski. "You do not have the power or the intelligence. I see nothing of myself in you."

"And I thank Anis for that. You have no hold over me. I am certain of my powers. I will not be dragged into your darkness." Then Yann said, in Romany, "You know your end."

He walked toward Kalliovski holding the shell as he would a shield. He stopped, and kneeling, laid the shell on Balthazar's body. As it touched him, the floor began to ripple, the center became a whirling vortex. Yann caught hold of Sido as the great dog was sucked down, down, down into the abyss.

Breaking the doom-filled silence that followed, Yann said, "Shall I tell you the story of the devil's dog?"

"What use have I for stories?"

"Every man who is foolish enough to do a deal with the devil is given a dog," said Yann as the threads of light began to dance from him. "The dog at first is his companion, but it grows with every evil deed his master does until it's of a size to take him down to meet the lord of the underworld."

Once again came a flicker on the flintstone of Kalliovski's mind, igniting a memory so bright, so intense that it seemed to wound him fatally.

"She told me that story," he said. "I thought she loved me. Anis told me that story."

Suddenly filled with rage, he threw the threads of darkness toward Yann. They fell, impotent, to the floor.

Thunder rolled from the bottom of the earth, as if hell's orchestra was tuning up, shaking the great chamber and rattling the walls of bone.

The floor began to ripple beneath Kalliovski as from the vortex rose the distant sound of Lucifer's anvil, and the panting of a great beast. Balthazar reappeared, quite transformed. His coat was burning flames of fury, his eyes the color of hot coals, his mouth dripping with molten saliva, scorching the ground.

Too late, Kalliovski remembered. "No, go back!" he screamed. "I didn't call for you!"

"But the devil did," said Yann.

Again Kalliovski threw the dark threads, but they were no defense against such a force as this. Balthazar clamped his jaws on the screaming figure of Kalliovski. In the intense heat, Kalliovski's face began to melt, the dark threads, flowing like Medusa's hair, trailed behind him as he was dragged down.

The devil's dog, the hound of hell, had come to take his master home.

Kalliovski's screams were drowned by the singing of the Seven Sisters Macabre, their ethereal voices ringing out:

> "Damask and death.
> Velvet and violence.
> Brocade and blood."

Still he fought with all that was left of his strength. His skeleton arm appeared. His hand clutched at Milkeye's ankle. Like a madman he tried to kick himself free of his master, but to no avail. He was pulled closer and closer to the edge. As he stood tottering on the brink, one of the Seven Sisters Macabre pushed him over.

The floor started to whirl again. Yann held on tightly to Sido as the walls of bone began to crumble. He knew they had to escape before the whole edifice collapsed.

One of the sisters put a hand out to stop him. "Only you can free us," she whispered. "Your survival depends on it."

"What must I do?"

"Call Balthazar."

Yann whistled for the dog, fearful that he was too late.

Then Balthazar emerged, no longer a monster, but the ghost of the puppy he had once been. Wagging his tail, he leaped up at Yann, and then jumped with joy at each of the Seven Sisters Macabre. Out of their battered and tortured carcasses emerged the ghosts of seven beautiful women, at long last set free, at long last at peace.

"Come with us," they beckoned.

Yann was conscious of a blinding light. Then he and Sido were in a meadow full of poppies, the Seven Sisters running through the tall grasses, laughing, chasing Balthazar toward the poplar trees.

Their voices sang out: "We are birds, we are free . . ."

Yann had no memory of how he got back to the the-ater. It was Basco, who, seeing what he thought were two ghosts, raised the alarm. Têtu came running down the stairs, a sword in his hand, to see Yann and Sido, covered in dust. At Sido's neck was the shell of shells.

That July morning a building in the rue des Couteaux collapsed into the catacombs. It had happened before; no doubt it would happen again. This time the disaster took only one shop. No one was quite sure how many were buried in the rubble. It was days later that they found the body of Serreto.

Chapter Thirty

Didier couldn't stand the noise of the prison. All night long it sounded like some grotesque engine fueled by fear. It gurgled, its belly rumbling, as if it were by degrees digesting its inmates. Just when he felt he had the measure of the infernal racket, he was wrong-footed by the voice of a woman singing. Her song rose, to be caught like a butterfly in an iron net.

In his windowless cell with no light, all Didier had for company were these voices.

He sat upright on the edge of his wooden bed, refusing sleep. It wasn't worth it; after all, he would be sent to his eternal rest soon enough.

At six in the morning, his cell was beginning to feel hot and airless. The iron grille in the door slid open and a clerk with ink-stained fingers pushed through a piece of paper with his indictment.

"Your trial's this afternoon."

Didier didn't bother to try to read it. He knew it was his death sentence.

The grille in the door still being open, he shouted for a guard. A man came limping, dragging his leg behind him. He had a kinder face than his fellow jailers.

"What is it, citizen?"

Didier handed him some money.

"Can you find out what's happened to a young man by the name of Yann Margoza? He was arrested with me last night."

"Keep your money," said the guard, and Didier thought he was going to walk away. Instead he said, "Yann Margoza? That name rings a bell. I once came across a lad with that name, working with a dwarf, if I remember correctly?"

"Perhaps. Why?" replied Didier, seeing a ray of hope. "Do you know him?"

"Yes and no. He never said his name, but afterward, I made inquiries."

"After what?"

"It was in the great winter of eighty-nine. Back then

I was a coachman. I worked for the Vicomtesse de Lisle. I gave a lad and a dwarf a lift back to Paris from the old de Villeduval estate. Saved my life, that boy did. I often wonder what happened to them two. Honorable. Not a word you can use much these days, but that's what those two Gypsies were. Honorable."

"That's Yann Margoza all right. How did he save your life?"

"The horses took fright on an icy road. Fireworks made them bolt. I thought we'd had it. The lad climbed down from the carriage, as bold as brass, and managed to mount one of the horses. He whispered into their ears, and blow me down if they didn't come to a halt. Yes, I tell you, I'd be a dead man if it weren't for Yann Margoza."

"Will you find out if he's here?" asked Didier.

"Leave it with me. My name's Dufort."

At half past two the door to Didier's cell was opened. He was taken through the wicket gates to a courtyard where fourteen prisoners were already walking up and down, a ragtag and bobtail collection of men. Ten were young wags, well dressed and well fed. They swanked around, bolstering themselves with fighting talk, each telling the other that he was innocent.

"I am a true revolutionary," said one.

"We'll be in Moët's Tavern before the day is done," said another.

"I shall be in my mistress's arms before the night is through," said a third.

Didier, always an observer, watched as one of their party boasted of what he would do when called before the public prosecutor.

"After all," he added, "it was I who designed the playing cards for the Republic."

The three priests took no notice of the young dilettantes. Neither did a man who looked mad, his beard white, almost down to his feet, with bits of straw and food in it, his clothes torn and tattered.

Didier breathed in the fresh air, tilting up his head, drawing down the sky. The prison courtyard was surrounded on all sides by the Conciergerie walls and the gothic towers of the Palace of Justice. Yet he could see a cockade of white sky high above, and he watched the swallows swooping, wishing with all his being that he too might sprout wings and fly.

Later that morning Didier, chained to his fellow prisoners, waited in the corridor. Fifteen prisoners in all to be seen by the judge in small groups. Didier, his back against the stone wall, waited for the first five to come out.

Dufort sidled up to him. "He's not here."

"But he must be," said Didier.

"A man took him away last night. Where to, they wouldn't say."

Dufort was interrupted by the sergeant. "What are you doing, talking to the prisoner?"

Dufort stood to attention. He sighed, looking along the line of men left waiting to be sent for trial. Were any of them guilty? He thought back to the days when he had worked for the viscountess. She would turn in her grave if she could see her old Dufort a guard in this most notorious of prisons. True, she was mean, stingy, and her monkey had been a pest. Yet for all that, when she died, just after the fall of the Bastille, she had left him her house to look after. As long as her monkey lived longer than four years, the house would be his. That was almost five years ago, and the monkey was still alive.

Dufort was a decent man. He wondered if Yann had been transferred to another prison, or already sent to the guillotine. If that was the case, he could at least do something to help the lad's friend.

Watching the sergeant walk away, he once more went up to Didier. "Where's the dwarf?"

"At the Circus of Follies in the Place de Manon."

Dufort had managed to get an hour off a day, pleading the needs of a child in his care. What he didn't say was that the child was a monkey. He liked to keep an eye on the viscount, as he called him, even though his wife was just as capable.

He made a detour to the Place de Manon, arriving at the theater out of breath, to find it apparently abandoned. He knocked on the stage door anyway. At last it was opened by Têtu, a huge sword in his hand.

"I'm a friend. I mean you no harm. I come from the Conciergerie. Didier told me where to find you. Please, we need to talk. My name is Dufort. I was a coachman for the Vicomtesse de Lisle."

Têtu looked at him, uncertain.

"Do you remember? I gave you a lift to Paris from the de Villeduval château, in the winter before the fall of the Bastille?"

Têtu was still studying him. "Yes," he said slowly. "I remember you."

"Yann Margoza saved my life that night, and I want

to repay the debt. Is there anything I can do to help you?"

"We need somewhere to hide."

"I have a house that no one will search. It is safe." He leaned forward. "It's the residence of the late viscountess."

Têtu put down the sword and shook Dufort's hand.

Yann appeared at the top of the stairs.

Dufort nodded. "Come with me," he said.

Didier was in the last batch of accused to be sent before the judge, who was an imposing sight, severe in his black hat and cloak with his dark hair and eyebrows.

"You," said the judge to the designer of cards, "you have a brother who is an aristocrat and an émigré."

"No, no, sir, I have no brother," replied the young man, seeing a glimmer of hope. There had, after all, been a misunderstanding. "I am an only child. I live with my mother, a widow."

"Quiet!" boomed the judge. "As I said, you have a brother and a father who are both émigrés and who have escaped to London, working for the British government."

The young man looked dumbfounded. "No, no, that's not—"

"Quiet!" shouted the judge, turning his attention to the next prisoner.

Didier had decided to say nothing. There was no justice here.

"Well, mooncalf, what have you to say in your defense?" said the judge. "You've been denounced as a traitor and a spy."

Seeing that Didier wasn't in the mood to argue his case, the judge moved on with relish to the poor man with the long white beard.

"Name?"

"The Duc de—"

The judge didn't even let him finish.

All of them were found guilty as charged.

Chapter Thirty-one

Basco, beside himself, was hardly aware of anything as he walked blindly along the street.

He as good as jumped out of his skin when someone grabbed his sleeve, and a man in a battered hat said, "Slow down, my friend."

"Yann," said Basco. "Oh, thank goodness."

Yann put his finger to his lips. "What has happened to Didier?"

"He was found guilty along with fourteen others. He has been condemned to death. They are taking him to the Place du Trône. We must do something."

"What about Citizen Aulard?"

"He's not on today's list," said Basco.

Yann and Basco mingled with the jeering crowd

across the Pont au Change, then through the rue de la Coutellerie to the Faubourg St. Antoine.

It had been Robespierre who had ordered the removal of the guillotine from the Place de la Révolution to the Place du Trône. His excuse for its removal was that it would waken the sleepier parts of Paris to the true meaning of the Terror. Those on the executioner's tumbrel had a longer, slower journey in which to contemplate the injustice of their sentences.

Didier, staring down from the cart, was unaware of his friends in the sea of faces. He stood taller than the rest of his companions in the tumbrel. Next to him was a girl who reminded Didier of a young deer, fresh faced, her whole life before her and about to be cut short. He heard her sob and say a "Hail Mary" under her breath.

"I'm frightened," she whispered. "They took my mother, and I can't see which cart she's in."

"Give the lady your seat," Didier said to the man sitting next to him.

"What's the point," he replied. "We're all dead."

"Listen to me. Look at that crowd. You know why they're jeering?"

"The same reason I jeered when I went to see the guillotine. They're grateful it's not them."

"Yes," said Didier, "and did you shout louder when you saw a man stumble, when a woman pissed herself?"

"For my sins, I did."

"And did you feel humbled when a man walked with his head held high and showed courage?"

"Yes."

"Then hold your head high, be proud that for the moment it's still connected to your body, and for the sake of this young terrified girl, be a man."

The procession continued its agonizingly slow journey. When they reached the rue du Faubourg St. Antoine, in sight of the Bastille, Didier looked up to see the sky darkening.

Yann and Basco had so far failed to attract his attention, and Yann was beginning to think that saving Didier might be beyond him, for the crowd was clumped together, a wall that seemed impossible to break through.

Suddenly the sky turned black, pitch-black. The gods were angry. Thunder rolled over Paris. Zeus sent lightning to rend the sky, and rain fell in huge gobbets, giant spitballs that bounced and burst in small puddles. The mob, frightened by the power of the elements, hurried for shelter in doorways and shopfronts.

Only Yann stood in the rain, soaking wet. Taking off his hat, his face illuminated as lightning flashed through the sky, he opened his long pale coat. In the eerie light it appeared incandescent, like butterfly wings.

Didier saw him then, silver in the storm, like an avenging angel, and his spirits rose.

Balling his huge hand into a fist he tipped back his head. I knew he wouldn't let me down. I knew it! He turned to the girl. "Don't give up hope. Keep praying."

The rain was still falling by the time the guillotine came into view. The stalwarts of the scaffold did not care about the weather, as long as heads fell as well. They had claimed their seats, waiting for the drama to begin.

The girl's cries could be heard loud and clear above the din of the storm as she called for her mother.

The guards, soaked through, took their places around the tumbrels. The executioner and his two attendants examined their human cargo. The executioner enjoyed making the most of their misery, for the crowd fed off the drama of these executions. The girl was exactly the kind of rosy plum he liked to begin with. He ordered the guard to pull her out. As she clung to Didier the guard wrenched her away. Didier had tears in his eye and a lump of fury in his throat. He would willingly kill all the guards, and the executioner.

"Be brave," he said as the girl was taken screaming from him.

A woman's voice cried, "Odette, where is my Odette?"

"*Maman*! Don't let me die!" the girl screamed. "Help me, someone, help me!"

"Come on," said the guard. "Let's get this young aristo executed. Bring the mother, let her watch."

Didier shouted to Yann, "Don't worry about me, save her!"

Basco eased himself closer to the tumbrels as the girl was brutally dragged to the scaffold, screaming, fighting, and kicking for all she was worth.

"Let's see," one of the old hags shouted.

The executioner tore off her hat.

"Oh, she's a piece of licorice if ever I saw one!" shouted one of her companions.

The girl, still sobbing, was tied to the plank.

The drums started to roll. The blade fell, to the

screams of the mother and the cheers of the onlookers, then came to a shuddering halt, less than a yard above the girl's head.

Yann, throwing his voice across the boom of the thunder, shouted, "Set the innocent free!"

The mob went silent, wondering what could have gone wrong.

Yann, his head aching, held tight the threads of light, keeping the silver blade fastened in midair.

Basco took his chance while the guards all had their heads turned toward the guillotine. He leaped onto the cart and cut the ropes tying Didier. Didier jumped down and, to a great cheer from the onlookers, pulled back the plank and untied the terrified girl. Yann could see that the guards were about to fire at Didier. He threw threads of light around them, pinning them down as Didier hoisted the girl over his shoulder. Basco, still on the tumbrel, cut the ropes of the other prisoners.

Only the executioner was free to examine his killing machine. Yann let go of the threads and the blade fell, too quickly for the executioner to remove his hand and in horror he stared at the stump, screaming in agony as his blood spurted over the knitting women.

In the chaos that followed, the prisoners clambered down the carts and ran to freedom. Some of the mob who tried to stop them found themselves pulled out of the crowd as if caught on a giant's fishing line, to be left hanging from the top of the guillotine like dead crows.

The mob was terrified. The old hags by the scaffold saw their knitting unravel. Hats flew off heads; swords fell out of their sheaths. The crowd began to disperse hurriedly. Was the Supreme Being sitting in judgment on them?

Rejoining Basco, Didier said, "We'd best get Yann and be gone."

Yann was so drunk with exhaustion that Didier had to prop him up.

"Is he all right?" said Basco.

"Yes. It takes its toll, working the threads of light," said Didier, setting off toward the Circus of Follies.

"Not that way," said Basco, "Yann told me we should go to the house of a Citizen Dufort."

"Dufort?" said Didier. "Well, I never."

"Têtu and Signorina Sido are there already," said Basco.

It didn't take them all that long to find the house, well hidden behind a rusty gate in a deserted street. If they hadn't known better, they would have thought that it had been long abandoned.

Têtu came out to greet them, followed by Dufort, who took them into the kitchen, where a meal was already laid and waiting.

"It's good to see you," said Dufort to Didier.

"I didn't imagine . . ." He stopped. "You're a good man, Dufort."

"Tell us what happened," said Têtu.

Didier started to relate the story.

Yann stood up, beginning to feel more like himself. "Têtu," he asked, "where is Sido?"

"Upstairs, sleeping."

Yann left the merry party to go find her.

The house was strangely preserved, wrapped up in huge dustsheets as if at any moment it would be brought back to life by tall-wigged, corseted women and elegant men.

Yann, uncertain of which way to go, spied a monkey in a wig and wearing full court dress. It jumped onto the shrouded furniture and sped toward him screeching, its teeth glimmering white. Then it stopped abruptly and banged on one of the doors in the corridor before running off.

As Yann watched it go, the door opened and there stood Sido. She threw her arms around him. "Oh, thank goodness, you are safe."

Whatever he had planned to say, to do, was lost the moment he saw her. He held her like a starving man and kissed her, not knowing how long it was since he had been this hungry, thinking it must have been years. He could feel her, feel her hunger as great as his. He knew then that there was an element beyond himself, a river, and he was weightless in its warm waters. He longed to understand its tides; pulled by its urgency, he was aware of the wave breaking, his whole being lost, drowning as it emerged breathless in another soul, knowing that this was the pull of the tide. This was the flow and the ebb. This was what love could do, transport you until you reached the sea, where the waves rise higher still, waiting, white-tipped and rolling. He was there and she was there and this was theirs and theirs alone, as if they were one, washed gently up on a longed-for distant shore, a land that would take a lifetime of togetherness to explore.

Chapter Thirty-two

Early the next morning Anselm arrived in the rue de la Culture Ste. Catherine. Colombine had hoped never to see him again, after what had happened at the Conciergerie.

He had been released along with the other actors, but everyone knew who was responsible for betraying Yann. Colombine had told Anselm that their marriage was over. Every one of the company had felt wretched, and Colombine, returning home, was disgusted with herself for being duped into turning traitor. Now here he was again with a mad, demonic glint in his eyes. His clothes were torn, his neckcloth filthy. He stank of drink.

She wanted to slam the door in his face, but he barged past her.

"Aren't you pleased to see me?" he said. "I've brought a friend with me, Mr. Tull."

Colombine took one look at the disheveled figure and recoiled.

"Don't he look a picture?" said Anselm, rummaging around to see if there was anything to drink. Finding a half-finished bottle, he tipped it down his throat so fast that wine dripped from his chin onto his waistcoat.

He went to kiss Colombine. His breath reeked of rotten fish.

Colombine pushed him away. "Get off me. I think you should leave and take that man with you."

"That's not very nice. That's no way to treat me, is it, Mr. Tull? And she's hurt your feelings, hasn't she?"

"Come on, Anselm. Let's get out of here. Has she got any money?"

"You heard him. Have you?"

"No. I have nothing. Just leave, for goodness' sake."

"You and me are in this together."

"Get off me."

"Oh no, Mr. Tull. She's cross with her Anselm. What shall we do with her?"

"Get out, both of you."

Anselm slapped her across the face. "Now, that's not nice." He pushed her up against the wall. "Have you seen Yann Margoza?"

"He's in prison, awaiting trial. That's what I heard."

"I wish that were so, but unfortunately you're wrong. Don't worry, though, I'm going to kill him for what he's done, before the day is out. Oh dear, a tear. Look, Mr. Tull, she's crying. Happy to see me at last."

"Leave her," said Mr. Tull. "We have bigger fish to catch."

Anselm still held her. "Give us a kiss good-bye, and tell Yann Margoza I will be waiting for him at the theater," he said. As Colombine turned her face from him, he punched her so hard it took her breath away.

She waited until they had gone before setting off in search of the only member of the theater company she knew might not wholeheartedly shun her.

Basco, sitting in his usual place in the Café de Foy in the Palais-Royal, was caught up in the middle of a heated debate.

"I tell you," said the waiter, "Robespierre shot himself, that's what I've heard, trying to avoid the guillotine."

"In the jaw? Why wouldn't he have done the job

properly? No, I think someone took a shot at him, a member of the National Assembly."

"Well, it don't matter," said the barman. "What matters is that he will be dead today without a trial, so I hear. They're moving the guillotine back to the Place de la Révolution so that everyone can see the bastard die."

"A tragedy," said the sans-culotte sitting at the table opposite. "A tragedy. France will be lost without him."

He stared into his glass. "Robespierre was a great man, a priest, a philosopher. You agree, citizen, don't you?" he said, addressing Basco.

"No, I don't," replied Basco. "I don't. I think he's a villain. I see nothing incorruptible about him. I see a villain who gets other men to carry out his murders."

"How can you say that?" said the sans-culotte. "He isn't responsible for what the tribunal decides."

"Do you want to fight? Do you? I am the great Basco!"

"Calm down, the pair of you," said the waiter.

The sans-culotte, seeing that he might well have met his match, shrugged his shoulders and mumbled under his breath, "You're wrong, the Republic will live to regret this day." He headed for the door and nearly bumped into Colombine.

Basco, pleased to have won his point and still fired up with the need for a fight, felt in the mood for giving Colombine the rough edge of his tongue. He was about to set to when he noticed the beads of sweat on her ashen face.

His fury began to fade as gallantry overtook him.

"Are you all right? You don't look well."

"I saw Anselm," she said, having trouble speaking. It was hurting to breathe. "I must have run too fast, I have a terrible stitch in my side. He's threatening to kill Yann . . . please, we must do something! He says he'll wait for Yann at the theater."

Basco noticed a small purple stain on her dress. As she talked, it began to spread.

Colombine, glancing down, saw it too and moved her hand there, lifting it to find it covered in blood. She looked horrified.

"Where's that come from?" she said, her eyes flashing in panic at the sudden realization of what Anselm had done.

Basco gently laid her on the floor, took off his coat, and rolled it up for a pillow.

"Get a surgeon. Now, man!" he said to the waiter.

"Don't leave me," said Colombine, clinging to his hand. "I don't want to die, don't let me die."

He pushed the hair out of her eyes.

"Shh, *bella ragazza,* it's all right."

Colombine, with tears spilling down her cheeks, said, "I did the right thing, coming here, didn't I?"

"Yes, *cara mia.* I will find him and tell him you came."

She lifted her fingers toward his face. Then her voice fell away with her hand.

The surgeon arrived soon after, but he was too late.

Colombine was already dead.

Basco, kneeling beside her, noticed that the surgeon had left his house wearing his slippers. Such a foolish thing, but the ordinariness of it was strangely comforting.

Outside, people were singing, celebrating the impending death of Robespierre. An impromptu band played. A man in an oddly old-fashioned hat went past, banging a child's drum and singing the Marseillaise.

A lad shouted in at the doorway, "This is a day to remember!"

Basco knew it was a day he would never forget.

Crossing himself, he bent down and closed Colombine's eyes.

He pulled himself together. There was no time to be lost. He must find Yann.

Yann lay in bed that late summer's morning, his limbs entwined with Sido's. He was lost to the season and the time of day. He became sleepily conscious when he heard someone tapping gently on the door. Careful not to wake Sido, he disentangled himself and, pulling on his breeches, went to the door.

"I'm sorry to disturb you," said Têtu, "but it's late."

Yann pulled the door behind him.

"Colombine has been murdered."

"By Anselm?" said Yann, saddened at the predictability of it.

Têtu nodded. "She found Basco before she died. She was desperate to warn you that Anselm is out to kill you too. He told Colombine he would wait for you at the theater."

Yann went back into the room and gathered his clothes. Sido lay lost in dreams, all sleepy like a meadow on a hot summer's day. Bending over her, he kissed her softly.

"I love you," he whispered.

Têtu was waiting at the top of the stone staircase as Yann quietly closed the chamber door.

"Didier should go with you," said Têtu, as if he had been giving the matter considerable thought.

"No," said Yann, "this is something I need to do on my own."

"It's too dangerous," said Têtu, following Yann down the stairs into the large cool marble hall.

"I owe you an apology," said Yann.

"You owe me nothing."

"I want you to know this."

"No, no, I don't need to know anything. I know it already."

"Will you be quiet, you old cantankerous dwarf, and let me say my piece?"

Têtu crossed his arms and stared belligerently at the opposite wall.

Yann laughed. "This is what I want you to know, just this and nothing more. I have a father, the best father I could ever have had; I have a friend, the best I could have had, and both these people are you, Têtu. It's because of you that I am who I am, and I would never have it differently."

"Being in love can make a man quite sentimental, you know," said Têtu curtly.

"I meant what I said."

"Cordell has sent word that arrangements are being made to take Sido back to London with all speed. I am to take her to him today."

"No," said Yann firmly. "You're taking her nowhere. She's staying with me. If Cordell wants to do anything, he can concentrate on getting Citizen Aulard out of prison. Do you understand?"

Têtu sighed. "Yes. I understand perfectly that Sido's aunt would be beside herself with anger if she knew what her niece had been up to."

Yann, unable to help himself, smiled. Regardless of Têtu's look of annoyance, he lifted him off his feet and kissed him on both cheeks. "If anything happens to me, you will look after Sido? If she wants, take her with you and Citizen Aulard to America . . ."

"Put me down. What on earth has come over you?" said Têtu, battling with an irritating wave of emotion that was making him feel grumpy. "Of course, and you know that."

"And you are not to let Cordell make any arrangements."

"I promise."

"Good. Tell me, old Gypsy, do I have Death on me today?"

Têtu said nothing.

"I do, don't I?"

Têtu's face was grave as he nodded. "Let's say he is close on your heels. Don't let him catch you, Yannick."

"Look after her, you bad-tempered old dwarf." The shadows drew in around Yann as Têtu watched him go. He closed the door and saw Sido standing at the top of the stairs. Panic rose in him. The talisman. Where was the talisman?

Holding on to the banister, she came down and, as if she had read his mind said, "It's all right. He has it safe on him."

348

Chapter Thirty-three

Citizen Aulard was freed from the Luxembourg prison the following day. He was quite baffled by the turn of events that had led to his safe delivery from the clutches of the tribunal. He had Iago to thank for his newfound freedom, for the parrot had spent his entire time in prison rousing the inmates and prison officers alike with his patriotic fervor and his whistling of the Marseillaise. It became apparent to all that Citizen Aulard was a man of the moment, a man of the Revolution, for anyone who had spent so much time training a parrot to speak like this could only be innocent of all charges.

His release had happened so quickly that it had gone unnoticed by Basco, whose job it was to keep an eye on the day's lists of those who were to be taken to the guillotine.

So it was that Citizen Aulard and Iago returned to the theater to find it deserted and, having not slept in ages, the good citizen lay down on his chaise longue. Both bird and man fell fast asleep.

Mr. Tull, creeping into the theater later that day, wasn't as set on the plan as Anselm. He was a man of limited imagination and couldn't see how it would be possible for Yann to teach Anselm those sort of tricks. After all, Anselm wasn't that bright. But whether he liked it or not, the lad had a point. They were broke, stony broke, for with the loss of his master went the loss of his income.

Mr. Tull had never been that keen on theaters. Places like this gave him the creeps—too many things to hide behind, too many ghosts. He felt better killing a man out in the open.

But Anselm was more than at home here. He knew exactly where to go and what he was looking for.

"Do you think he will come?" asked Mr. Tull.

"Oh, he'll come all right."

"Why?"

"Because I killed Colombine."

At first Mr. Tull wasn't sure he had heard right. "No, you didn't. She was alive when we left her."

Anselm, his face shining, said, "I didn't work with Butcher Loup without learning where to put the knife in. Let's just say he'll come."

"What's that noise?"

"Shush," said Anselm.

They waited in a dark recess.

Citizen Aulard had woken and thinking he heard voices, wandered down to the stage, hopeful of seeing Têtu. Instead, there before him, looking quite deranged, stood Anselm.

Yann had not been expecting anyone else at the theater apart from Anselm. He walked onto the stage to find him with a pistol in his hand and a knife in his belt, his eyes flickering. Then he saw Mr. Tull twisting Citizen Aulard's arm up his back and holding a gun to his head.

"If you do any of your magic tricks," said Anselm, his feverish eyes on Yann, "Mr. Tull here will kill him. I mean it."

"What is it you want with me?" asked Yann.

"What do you think? I want what's mine, to know

how the threads of light work. You see," said Anselm, coming closer, "Count Kalliovski meant me to have the gift of the threads of light. He promised as much. It doesn't belong to you. Do you know why?"

Yann said nothing.

"Well, then, I'll tell you. Because I know I'm his son. He didn't realize it, but I know. I heard voices, they told me it was so. They are telling me now. I am his rightful son and heir, not you."

"Hold on a mo," said Mr. Tull. "What are you rambling on about? He didn't have a son."

"Shut up, Tull. I ain't speaking to you."

"I was born with the gift," said Yann slowly, all the time thinking how to get Citizen Aulard out of this alive. "My magic belongs to the light."

"I'm getting very angry," said Anselm, "aren't I, Mr. Tull? He isn't hearing what I'm saying, is he?"

"That's right," replied the old rogue, his eyes glued to his worrying erstwhile protégé.

Yann looked at Citizen Aulard and said calmly, "I'm glad to see they released you."

"I'm so sorry, I should have—"

"Shut your mouths," said Anselm. "Come on. Unless you tell me the secret of your magic, I'll kill him."

"Let him go."

Anselm burst out laughing. "Got you now, haven't I?"

He pulled back the trigger and pointed his weapon straight at Citizen Aulard's heart. "His death will be your fault."

Mr. Tull, seeing what Anselm was about to do, yelled, "Wait a minute—I'm holding him!"

"Well, don't!" shouted Anselm.

At that moment, as Mr. Tull let go of Citizen Aulard, Iago flew onto the stage, straight at the startled Anselm. His pistol went off.

Yann saw the smoke and, for a fraction of a second, relived the nightmare that had haunted him since boyhood, the moment the old magician Topolain had failed to catch the bullet. He concentrated all his powers and reached with his mind's eye for the missile.

Yann looked at his hand. It was covered in blood, but he had caught the bullet.

Citizen Aulard stumbled into the darkness backstage. As Anselm reloaded, Yann threw out the threads of light to catch the pistol, missing his target as Anselm darted up the stairs to the fly tower. There among the ropes and lanterns he looked down on the stage, took aim at Yann, and fired. To his astonishment, his second bullet found its mark in Mr. Tull's shoulder.

Yann followed Anselm up to the fly tower. He flicked out the threads of light and, lifting him off his feet, hung him like a pendulum above the stage.

Mr. Tull rose unsteadily, murder glittering in his eyes. He had had enough, more than enough of Anselm Loup. Seeing him hovering there, he knew what he was going to do.

"Get me down, Tull," shouted Anselm.

Mr. Tull pulled back the trigger and fired his pistol at Anselm's rotten heart.

Every citizen in Paris would be able to tell you exactly where they were on the day of Robespierre's execution. Paris was in a holiday mood. The streets hummed with people. There was an air of excitement. The Terror was ending and France stood at the dawn of a new era. The two lovers, oblivious to everything but each other, walked, hand in hand, against the tide of the crowd. At the Jardin du Luxembourg they strolled along a winding gravel path.

"Without the Revolution," said Yann as they sat under a grove of chestnut trees, "we would never have been together, and I wouldn't be able to ask you this. Will you marry me?"

Sido, her blue eyes shining, said, "With all my heart, yes."

"Even if your aunt and uncle don't give their consent?"

"Yes. As long as you promise me we won't have an ordinary life, and that whatever we do, we'll do it together."

He laughed and, wrapping her in his arms, kissed her.

"It will be filled with adventures. This is the just the beginning, I promise."

Chapter Thirty-four

Henry Laxton sat in his study in Queen Square, having just finished reading the letters that had arrived that morning from Paris. Leaning back in his chair, he looked out of the study window at the sun-dappled leaves of the oak tree in the garden and remembered the day he had first seen Yann. Who would have thought then . . . ? Oh, well. Life is a strange affair.

Among the letters, one had finally arrived from The Travelers' Arms. It was not, as the writer, a Mr. Suter, reported, the cleanest of inns. Hence he believed that the letter he had found might have gone undiscovered for longer still, if it hadn't been for the fact that he had taken a room at the inn to recover from the effects of seasickness. Seeing the painting of the galleon upon a wild sea, he had turned the picture to face the wall. In doing so, he dislodged Sido's letter. Being an honest man, Mr. Suter had posted it, and he hoped that whatever the letter had to say, it hadn't arrived too late to be of use.

It contained a hurried and frightened note from Sido. A few weeks ago this note would have brought Henry comfort, but now the circumstances were well known to him and his wife. Poor Juliette had suffered badly, and her condition had not improved when she heard that her niece had no intention of returning to London before her wedding. A wedding that Juliette still believed to be ill-advised.

Now Cordell's letter outlined the situation perfectly. Regardless of any objections her aunt might have, Yann and Sido were to be married, and there would be another revolution if anyone tried stop them. He added that in his humble opinion Sido could do no better.

Were it not for Yann, there would be many Frenchmen and women from all walks of life who would not be alive today.

He is a young man with a future, and I hope we can persuade him to employ his extraordinary talents and bravery on our behalf in the years to come.

To the matter of Mr. Tull, Kalliovski's agent in London
and Paris: He was arrested for the murder of Anselm Loup
and sent to the guillotine four days after Robespierre,
convicted as an English spy.

The next letter was from Yann.

Dear Mr. Laxton,

I know very well that I am not the one Mrs. Laxton
would have desired for her niece, and perhaps you too
would have wanted someone better. I have loved Sido
since I first saw her all those years ago in the Marquis de
Villeduval's château. I loved her before I knew what love
was.

I know in my heart that I am a ghost-child of my
mother's one true love. His spirit is in me. My father,
the father who raised me and deserves the name, is an
extraordinary man named Têtu. I have so much for which
to thank him: for the courage he has given me, the love
that has surrounded me, and a feeling of home without the
inconvenience of four walls.

I promise to look after Sido, to honor her, to love her.
She is my soul, she is my life. We will walk together
always.

Fortune smiles kindly on us. I pray that you will too.
Your blessing on our marriage would mean a great deal to
us both.

It was a very humble and truthful letter and had moved
Henry deeply.

The last one had again been from Sido.

My dear aunt and uncle,

I am sure by now you have been told that I am well and
happier than I have ever been. Yann, I know, has written
to ask for your blessing and I hope with all my heart that
you will be able to give it.

No doubt, Aunt, you are upset, and wish I was
marrying someone of my own rank, but the man I am
betrothed to is of noble birth. He was born to be King of the
Gypsies.

We will go to America to start our married life, to begin
again. I truly believe this is for the best. Têtu is coming
with us, as is Monsieur Aulard, with a view to opening a
theater for magic.

Always your affectionate niece,

Sido

Henry was greatly relieved. In his heart of hearts he knew the young lovers would do well.

Putting down his glasses, he looked up to see that tea was being served in the garden and he felt somewhat sheepish. If he had been honest with Juliette, and told her Yann hadn't gone back to Paris to be an actor, if he had told her who the Silver Blade was, would she have fewer objections to the marriage?

Vane came into the room. "Mrs. Laxton is asking that you join her, sir."

Henry stood up and, walking out into the garden, prepared to tell his wife an extraordinary story.

Epilogue

It was on a mellow September afternoon, as the mist once more clung like a lady's mantle to the earth and the air was filled with the smell of a passing summer, that the wedding of Yann Margoza and Sidonie de Villeduval took place in Normandy at the château of the Duchesse de Bourcy.

The long table in the dining room had been laid with the best silver and plates, and the candelabras lit so that the chamber had the quality of sun-filled honey as the guests filtered in.

Henry Laxton had chartered a private boat from Brighton to bring over Juliette, Mr. Trippen, the Duc de Bourcy and his two sons. It had been an emotional reunion for everyone, each for different reasons. Juliette, who had decided to put aside all her objections to the marriage, found herself humbled by the change in her niece and bewildered by her beauty. Cordell had arranged for the actors from the Circus of Follies to be brought from Paris. Monsieur Aulard, sitting next to Têtu, was excited by the future. In two days' time, he,

Têtu, and Monsieur and Madame Margoza would be sailing for New York. Oh, he thought, how the world has tumbled upside down to land on its feet again.

Didier was sitting with Dufort and the monkey, "the viscount," who was remarkably well behaved and well dressed. Basco was in his element talking to Juliette.

Têtu, silently observing the proceedings, could see in the flickering light of the candles that the spirits were watching them. Anis, with Manouche by her side, was there to give her blessing.

The champagne flowed and, as the great doors opened and the little collection of musicians began to play, everyone stood, glasses raised.

"To Monsieur and Madame Margoza!"

Yann saw the threads of light spinning around them, all silvery, diamond, ruby bright, and knew that shadows were but passing clouds. Putting his hands to Sido's face he kissed her.

She said softly, "We are birds . . ."

Yann smiled. "We are the children of the Revolution, We are free."

Acknowledgments

I would like to thank Judith Elliott for her help in finishing the first draft. Thanks too, to the wonderful Jacky Bateman, who puts up with the vilest spelling mistakes and still manages to laugh, for her long-suffering patience during the many rewrites. There are, as she says, three ghost books from which this one has emerged.

My grateful thanks to Fiona Kennedy, who helped shape the novel, pulling all the strands of the story together and weaving a better book; to Lauri Hornik at Dial Books for her continuing support; to my agent, Rosemary Sandberg; and last but not least to the girl I met on a school visit who shyly asked, "Please Miss, when will you write more romance—like Mr. Rochester in *Jane Eyre*?"

I hope I understood the question. This book is my answer.

—SG